"We can work it out," Ricardo said.

"I'm older, more understanding of the way you feel. I'm still passionate about what I do, that hasn't changed, but I'm not as hot-blooded as I was."

"Aren't you?"

He grinned, understanding Rebecca. "When I am with you, my blood is as hot as it was when I was a teenager. I wish I had known you then. I wish I had spent every day of my life with you." He leaned across the table and in an impassioned voice said, "I wish now I had refused to let you leave me. I wish I had locked you in a room and kept you there, because I have hated every moment that we've been apart, every night that we haven't made love, every morning that I have awakened without you beside me."

"Ricardo—"

"I won't let you go again. Not after last night. You said you loved me, Becky. How can I let you go again after that?" He brought her hand to his lips.

Dear Reader,

We've got a terrific lineup of books for you this month
something I hope you've come to expect from
Silhouette Intimate Moments. Starting off with a bang,
Anne Stuart makes her second appearance in the line
with *Now You See Him . . .*. This is a hair-raisingly
suspenseful look at the struggle of Francey Neeley to
recover from the heartbreak and betrayal inflicted on
her by a man who turned out to be a coldhearted
terrorist. Complicating her life is the arrival of Michael
Dowd, a man who may or may not be the good guy and
romantic savior he seems. You'll be turning pages long
into the night once you pick up this book!

Two of our "February Frolics" authors are back this
month, too. Rachel Lee makes her third appearance
with *Defying Gravity,* while Rebecca Daniels offers
L.A. Midnight, a sequel to her first book, *L.A. Heat.*
Both of these talented writers have created characters
who will find their way into your heart forever. Finally,
Barbara Faith's *The Matador* is a story of love regained
and a family rebuilt, when a long-estranged couple find
the power to overcome their differences in the face of
what may be a life-ending injury to *the matador.*

In coming months, more of your favorite authors will
be appearing, including Nora Roberts in June, and
Marilyn Pappano and Paula Detmer Riggs in July. And
that's only a taste of what's to come, so be here every
month for the best in romance today, especially for you
from Silhouette Intimate Moments.

Yours,
Leslie Wainger
Senior Editor and Editorial Coordinator

BARBARA FAITH

The Matador

SILHOUETTE·INTIMATE·MOMENTS®

Published by Silhouette Books New York

America's Publisher of Contemporary Romance

SILHOUETTE BOOKS
300 East 42nd St., New York, N.Y. 10017

THE MATADOR

Copyright © 1992 by Barbara Faith

ISBN: 0-373-07432-8

First Silhouette Books printing May 1992

Printed in the U.S.A.

Books by Barbara Faith

Silhouette Intimate Moments

The Promise of Summer #16
Wind Whispers #47
Bedouin Bride #63
Awake to Splendor #101
Islands in Turquoise #124
Tomorrow Is Forever #140
Sing Me a Lovesong #146
Desert Song #173
Kiss of the Dragon #193
Asking for Trouble #208
Beyond Forever #244
Flower of the Desert #262
In a Rebel's Arms #277
Capricorn Moon #306
Danger in Paradise #332
Lord of the Desert #361
The Matador #432

Silhouette Special Edition

Return to Summer #335
Say Hello Again #436
Heather on the Hill #533
Choices of the Heart #615
Echoes of Summer #650
Mr. Macho Meets His Match #715

Silhouette Desire

Lion of the Desert #670

Silhouette Books

Silhouette Summer Sizzlers 1988
"Fiesta!"

BARBARA FAITH

is a true romantic who believes that love is a rare and precious gift. She has an endless fascination with the attraction a man and a woman from different cultures and backgrounds have for each other. She considers herself a good example of such an attraction because she has been happily married for twenty years to an ex-matador she met when she lived in Mexico.

"The glittering festival of courage,
   Terror, and delight,
   Of this proud and ancient people . . .
   Gold and silk and blood and sun!"

—Manuel Machado

"No, I do not love the bullfight, but I love the bull,
   and I love the man who reassures to us that we are of
   the race of men."

—John Steinbeck

He told me once that bullfighting was a passion that
   he would never get out of his system.
   "It was everything," he said. "It was
   all that mattered."
And I said, "If we had met earlier and I had asked
   you to give it up for me, would you have?"
He looked at me, surprised by my question.
   But he did not answer.
In spite of that unanswered question, Alfonso,
   or perhaps because of it,
   this book is dedicated to you.
   With love.

Chapter 1

The phone call came ten minutes after midnight.

"Ricardo's been hurt," Isabel said in Spanish. "At the corrida in Mexico City today. It's bad, Megan. The doctors aren't sure he's going to make it. They said..." Her voice broke. "He's been asking for you. I... I know it's been a long time. I know I shouldn't ask... but if you could come..."

Ricardo. Hurt. Asking for her. Oh, God. Oh, please, God. She clutched the receiver, hard, so that she wouldn't drop it. "Of course, I'll come."

"Can you bring Pilar with you? In case..." Isabel began to cry.

Megan fought for control. "Yes, I'll bring her," she managed to say.

"Tomorrow?"

Megan looked at the clock over the refrigerator. "Today," she said.

After she put the receiver down, she stood there beside it, frozen. This was the moment she had always feared. She had thought that if she could remove herself from him, that if she were two thousand miles away when it happened, the pain wouldn't be as sharp or as deep. But she had been wrong.

Fist against her mouth so that she wouldn't cry out, Megan barely managed to smother a moan. She grabbed the edge of the kitchen sink and bent double as though she, too, had been wounded.

"Ricardo," she whispered. "Oh, Ricardo."

She took a deep breath and picked up the phone. Three calls later she had two seats on a flight that left Miami International at eight-thirty.

Silently then, so as not to wake her daughter, Megan went out onto the porch and down the steps that led to the dock. The night was quiet, the sea was calm, and though it was November the air was hot and still. Water splashed against the hull of the boats as she walked toward the end of the dock. A sleepy pelican opened yellow eyes and blinked at her from his position atop one of the posts.

And finally, alone, where she wouldn't awaken Pilar or any of the guests staying at her motel, Megan let the tears come. Tears for Ricardo, for what had been and was no more. She cried for a long time, and when she dried her tears, she gazed out over the clean, calm water.

Key Largo had been her and Pilar's home for five years. It was where she had come to escape from Mexico and from the memory of Ricardo.

But memories had a way of catching up to you, and it seemed to Megan as she sat alone in the quiet night that she could see and remember exactly the way it had been that long-ago summer in Mexico.

Some women matured at twenty-one, but Megan wasn't one of them, which was probably the reason her parents didn't want her to go to Mexico the summer of her senior year at the University of Miami.

"But I'm a Spanish major," Megan argued. "I'll be going to school every day and living with a Mexican family. Professor Shaw and his wife are chaperoning the group. There's absolutely nothing to worry about."

At last her parents consented, and it turned out to be the happiest summer of Megan's life.

She knew it would be from the moment she saw San Rafael. In the heartland of Mexico, four hours northwest of Mexico City, it lay on a mountainous plateau almost seven thousand feet above sea level. She got out of the bus when it stopped at a mirador overlooking the town, and while the other students talked excitedly she stood, spellbound.

San Rafael was a fairy-tale town of steepled Spanish colonial churches, old stone buildings and cobblestone streets. In the distance she saw the rise of mountains and fields of yellow wildflowers. From below she heard the bells, sonorous and solemn, calling out to the faithful. An old man leading three burros laden with firewood stopped for a moment to listen, then went on his way down one of the narrow cobbled streets. From the small house across the road came the smell of wood smoke and roasting corn.

Megan stood silently, moved as she had never been before, and she knew somewhere deep inside her that this was a very special place and that this would be a very special summer.

She boarded with a family by the name of Chavez in a lovely old home three blocks off the central plaza. In addition to Señor Chavez and his wife there were four young children—Clemente, Marimar, Gerardo and Juanita—as well as an elderly grandfather and a maiden aunt whose name was Hermalinda. None of them spoke English.

The first week was difficult for Megan because she was too shy to say more than a few words in Spanish. But by the second week she forgot her shyness and was able to talk with everyone in the family and to look forward to the midday *comida* when they were all together.

She enjoyed school. Her teacher, Isabel Montoya, was only a few years older than Megan. A small, vivacious woman, only an inch over five feet, she had short, curly hair, Spanish green eyes and a nonstop personality. She had studied at the University of Miami four years before Megan, and she and Megan had had some of the same professors. Because they had that in common, and because they liked each other almost immediately, they became friends.

"We're having a *tienta* this weekend at the ranch," Isabel said one afternoon after class. "That's when we test young bulls and the cows that will be used in breeding our brave bulls. It's a serious business, but it's fun, too. I'd like you to come so that you can meet my family." She grinned. "Especially my brother. Ricardo's twenty-five and a matador. One of the best. Next season he's going to be fighting in Spain. Our father's there now arranging his schedule."

A bullfighter? Megan hadn't been sure how she felt about that. She'd seen *Blood and Sand* on the late, late show a couple of years ago. She'd thought Tyrone Power was handsome and that both Linda Darnell and Rita Hayworth were beautiful. But she hadn't liked the bullfighting scenes, so when Isabel asked her to go to the *tienta,* she hesitated.

"It'll be fun," Isabel insisted. "Please, Megan, I want you to come."

And it was fun.

The guests were already gathered in the *tentadero,* the family bullring, when Isabel and Megan arrived. A few of the older men were seated there, but others stood behind the red wooden wall that formed the small ring. Almost all of the men were dressed in what Isabel told her were *traje de corto,* tight pants that fitted into fine Spanish boots, short tight jackets and white ruffled shirts.

One of them was tall and slim and looked as though he had been poured into the gray pants and short black jacket.

"That's Ricardo," Isabel said when she saw Megan watching him. "Come on, I'll introduce you." They walked over and Isabel tapped him on his shoulder. "Ricardo," she said. "I want you to meet my friend, Megan Quinn."

He turned and looked at Megan. A slight smile curved his wickedly full lips. *"Mucho gusto,"* he said, and enclosed her hand in his. "You're the student Isabel has told me about. Yes?"

Mesmerized by the intensity of his golden amber eyes, Megan could only nod.

"I hope you'll enjoy the *tienta*. Afterward there will be music and dancing. You must save me a dance. Yes?"

This time she managed an answer, "Yes," before she turned to follow Isabel up to a seat above the small bullring.

The guests grew silent. The picador, mounted on a padded horse, rode into the ring. A man called out, *"¡Puerta!"* A door was thrown open, and a cow, long, thin, razor-sharp horns glinting in the sun, raced into the ring where the picador waited. She headed straight to the horse, received only a small pic, charged again, then Ricardo stepped into the ring.

Megan watched, breathless with excitement. She had never seen a man display such grace of movement, such calmness in the face of danger. Four hundred years ago he would have been a gladiator or a knight at King Arthur's court. Today he was a matador, a fighter of bulls, a man from the top of his crisp black hair to his expensive Spanish boots. His movements were precise, and there was about him a cool, barely controlled passion that both frightened and excited her.

He tested animal after animal, furling the red cape as he brought each one close to his lean, hard body. It was like a ballet, Megan thought, a dangerous, risk-taking ballet, a duel between a slim young man whose only protection was a piece of cloth, and an animal with stiletto-like horns.

Other men took a turn with the cape, but it was Ricardo who dominated the day, Ricardo who, even to Megan's inexperienced eyes, was so much better than the others.

Later, after the serious business of the testing was completed, some of the guests tried their hand with the smaller cows. Still later everyone moved to the flower-filled patio of the family home where tables had been set up.

A large table near the center fountain displayed a wonderful variety of food: rare roast beef, country ham, chorizo, tamales, tacos, varieties of cheeses and sausages, tortillas and fresh, crusty *bolillos*. At the other end of the table there were bowls of ripe strawberries, slices of watermelon, papaya and mango. And bottles of red Spanish wine.

A mariachi band played and a few couples danced.

"Having fun?" Isabel asked.

"This is wonderful!" Megan answered. "Thank you for inviting me." She glanced over to the table where Ricardo sat surrounded by his friends and women who were clustered around him like a colorful array of bright summer flowers. He looked up and raised his glass of wine. But it wasn't until the afternoon had waned and the soft colors of twilight softened the sky that he came to where Isabel and Megan were sitting.

He kissed his sister's cheek, then, reaching for Megan's hand, he said, "We will dance. Yes?"

He led her toward the old stone fountain where water splashed and he asked, as Isabel had, if she had enjoyed the day.

"Yes," Megan said. "Oh, yes."

He put his arms around her, and they began to dance to the music of a Mexican waltz. He was almost a foot taller than she was, and though he was slender, his shoulders were broad. He had showered and changed after the *tienta,* and now he was dressed in a soft cashmere sweater and tailored gray pants.

He intimidated her; she simply didn't know what to say to him. He asked, "How old are you?"

She looked up at him, surprised by the question. "Twenty-one," she finally replied.

"Twenty-one?" He frowned. "How is it that your parents allowed you to come to Mexico alone?"

"I'm not alone." She met his frown with one of her own. "I came with a group from the university. We're very properly chaperoned, Señor Montoya."

"A Mexican girl of your age wouldn't be allowed to visit a neighboring town by herself, let alone another country," he said.

"I'm not a girl," Megan snapped. "I'm a woman. An American woman."

A reluctant smile curved his mouth. "Yes, you are, aren't you?"

She knew he had only asked her to dance because she was a friend of Isabel's, but now, suddenly, she saw a flash of interest in his eyes, eyes that were fringed with indecently long dark lashes.

Earlier today she had wished she had dressed, like the other women, in jeans or tailored pants and boots. Now, because of the way Ricardo was looking at her, she was glad she'd worn her blue dress.

His arms tightened around her. "Where are you staying?"

She looked up at him in surprise. "With the Chavez family on Reloj Street."

"Do they allow you to date?"

Allow? There was that word again, and it made her angry. "I'm not here to date," she said with some asperity. "I'm here to study Spanish."

"If you really wish to learn, you need to go out more."

He smiled, and she felt a strange, sudden urge to touch his mouth.

"With me," he added.

Her heart made a strange little jump.

"Tomorrow night. I'll speak to Señora Chavez. I know the family and I'm sure it will be all right." He tucked a strand of hair behind Megan's ear. "Yes?"

She let out the breath she didn't know she'd been holding. She wanted to draw herself up to her full five feet four inches and say that indeed she wouldn't. Instead she said yes.

And that was how it began.

"Look, Mom!" Seven-year-old Pilar pressed her nose against the window of the plane and looked at the city below. "How come it's so cloudy?"

"That's smog, honey. Twenty million people live down there, and at least half of them are driving cars."

"Was there smog when we lived here? I don't remember anything."

"We didn't live in Mexico City, Pilar. We lived at your grandfather's ranch. That's near San Rafael, the town where I went to school."

"And where you met Daddy." Eyes so like Ricardo's looked up at her. "Will we go there, Mom, or are we just going to Mexico City?"

"It depends on how your dad is, Pilar. If there's time, then, yes, we can go to San Rafael. It's a beautiful place, I'd like you to see it."

"Did Aunt Isabel say that Dad was hurt real bad? He isn't going to die, is he?"

Megan hesitated, but before she could say anything one of the attendants came on to announce they were making the final approach to Mexico City.

"Fasten your seat belts and be sure your seats are in an upright position," the attendant said, and the plane drifted down through the clouds and at last touched the runway.

"Is Aunt Isabel going to meet us?" Pilar asked.

Megan nodded, glad now that she and Isabel had kept in touch through the years and that two years ago Isabel had come to Key Largo to visit. She and Pilar had gotten acquainted, and it had given Pilar a feeling of her other family, her Mexican family.

But though Pilar knew her father's sister, she hadn't seen her father since she had left Mexico five years ago. Now, as she had so many times before, Megan wondered if she and Ricardo had made the right decision when they separated.

There had been such bitterness in parting, and so much pain. On that final day Ricardo's face had been uncharacteristically hard and unyielding, his voice firm, uncompromising.

"I want Pilar to know who she is," he had said. "I don't want her to grow up questioning whether she's Mexican or American and feeling guilty because her loyalties are divided between the two of us. I won't settle for an occasional weekend or a month in the summer. It has to be all or nothing, Megan, for both you and Pilar."

"You're right," she'd said. "It's better this way."

His jaw had tightened, and without a word he'd picked Pilar up from her stroller and walked out to the waiting car. That had been the last time Megan and Pilar had seen him, but every Christmas, every birthday, Easter and Valentine's Day, Pilar had received gifts from him. And every month since they had separated a check had been deposited in Megan's Florida bank.

Whenever Pilar had asked about her father, Megan had told her that he was a fine, wonderful man. "He lives half of the year in Mexico and half in Spain. That's why he isn't able to see you," she'd explained. "But he loves you very much, darling. Always remember that."

Megan had shown Pilar pictures of Ricardo and once, when she'd gotten older, Pilar had said, "I'm sorta a combination, aren't I? I mean, I look kinda like Daddy and kinda like you."

And it was true: Pilar had eyes exactly like Ricardo's and her skin was the same golden sand color. But she was small-boned and delicate, like Megan, and her hair was the same shade of pale golden blond.

There had been so many times over the years when Megan had asked herself if she and Ricardo had been right in thinking they were doing what was best for Pilar. And she wondered, too, if they should have divorced instead of deciding on a legal separation.

And there were painful times when she wondered if she should have stayed with Ricardo, days and nights when she longed for him, and for Mexico. For though she loved Florida, she missed the warmth and color of Mexico.

She was proud, though, of what she had accomplished. When she first bought the Gaviota Motel, it had been a run-down, ramshackle fishermen's weekend retreat. Now it was one of the most popular small resorts in the Florida Keys, a laid-back, comfortable place where snowbirds from the north came to escape the cold and bustle of big-city life.

People from Miami, Fort Lauderdale and other parts of Florida came, too. Many of them brought their boats down and stayed for a weekend, a week, a month, a few for the whole winter.

It was a place where people didn't have to dress up, where blue jeans, cutoffs and bathing suits were de rigueur, where guests dined on catfish, shrimp, stone crabs and hush puppies prepared by a cook named Delilah. It was a happy place, and Megan had been happy there.

Megan had told herself that she had all but forgotten ever having been married to Ricardo, ever having loved him, but she had known when she replaced the telephone receiver last night that she hadn't forgotten one moment of the three years they had been together.

Isabel was waiting for them when they cleared customs. She hugged Megan, then gathered Pilar into her arms. "Just look at you, *muchacha,*" she said. "I can't believe how you've grown. You're beautiful!"

Pilar blushed with pleasure. "How's my dad?" she asked when she stepped away.

"He's not doing too well, *querida,* but he has two very good doctors, and they're working hard to make him better."

"*¿Verdad?* Is that true?" Megan asked.

Isabel nodded. "He's been badly hurt," she said when Pilar turned away for a moment. "But the doctors are hopeful." She motioned for a helper, and when their bags were picked up, she said, "I thought you'd like to go right to the hospital, Megan. I'll drop you off and take Pilar home with me."

"I want to see him, too." Pilar firmed her chin and glared at her aunt with an expression so like Ricardo's when he was angry that Isabel laughed and hugged the little girl to her.

"You'll see him later, *muchacha*," Isabel said. "Right now it's best that you come home with me."

"But—"

"No buts, Pilar," Megan said firmly. "You can see your father as soon as he's feeling better. I promise."

Once in the car, she turned to Isabel and asked, "What about Franco? Does he know I'm coming?"

Isabel shook her head, but she didn't answer until she had maneuvered the car out of the airport parking lot and they were on the *autopista*. "He hasn't left Ricardo's side since it happened," she said then. "This morning Mama and I were able to talk him into going back to the ranch so that you could be alone with Ricardo. I . . ." She swerved out of the way of an old, multidented car, leaned on her horn and yelled a Spanish curse that Megan hadn't heard in the five years she'd been away. "I didn't tell Papa you were coming," Isabel went on. "But you'll have to see him if you plan to stay at the hospital."

"I plan to stay. How is he?"

"Older." Isabel shook her head. "And tougher."

"He won't be happy to see me."

"No, he won't."

"How's your mother?"

"Mama's fine. I told her you were coming, and she told me to tell you that she was glad you were. She always liked you, Megan, but she thought you were wrong to leave."

"Did you?"

Isabel shrugged. "I did at first, but after a while I realized how hard everything had been for you, and I understood why you went away."

"Do you think Ricardo ever understood?"

Isabel pulled up to the entrance of the hospital and stopped. "No," she said. "He never did."

Chapter 2

Megan hesitated in front of the door to Ricardo's room, unsure whether to knock or go in, when the door opened and a nurse came out. Eyebrows raised, and she looked at Megan and asked in Spanish, "Can I help you?"

"I . . . I came to see Señor Montoya," Megan said.

"Are you a relative?"

"I'm his wife."

"I didn't know Señor Montoya was married."

"I've been away," Megan said. "I've just returned. How is he?"

"His condition is stable. The doctor will be in later. It is best you speak to him, Señora Montoya."

Señora Montoya. Megan took a deep breath and pushed the door open. When it closed behind her, she leaned against it for a moment as she looked down at the bed where he lay. His face was drawn, and there were lines that hadn't been there before, as well as a scar that ran from one corner of his mouth to his chin.

She moved a chair closer to the bed and sat beside him. "Ricardo?" she asked softly, and began to stroke the hair back from his forehead. "It's Meggie," she whispered. "I'm here, Ricardo. I won't leave you now."

Nurses came and went. A doctor looked at Ricardo's chart, nodded to Megan but didn't speak. Afternoon faded into evening, and still she sat there beside his bed, speaking softly, holding his hand. Often she touched the simple wide gold band on her finger, the ring that Ricardo had placed there that long-ago day when they promised to love each other forever. And she remembered the way it had been.

That first night at dinner she was awkward and unsure of herself, but Ricardo was as poised and in control as a man twice his age.

The restaurant he took her to was up in the mountains, a half-hour drive from San Rafael. It was an elegant, charming place, and because the night was warm they were led to a table on the patio. There was candlelight and wine, and a guitarist who played old Mexican songs.

Ricardo was the perfect date, pleasant and attentive, and so good-looking that she had trouble concentrating on her food. He ordered warm tortillas with country cheese and salsa for an appetizer, and when it came, he prepared a tortilla for her and held it to her lips for her to taste. And when he wiped a dab of salsa from the corner of her mouth he let his finger trail across her lips in a lingering caress.

Her lips trembled at his touch. He smiled gently and began to tell her about the bulls and what it was like to fight them.

"I'm going to go to Spain at the end of next month," he said. "My father has fights scheduled for me in Madrid, Sevilla and Granada. I've never been to Spain and I'm looking forward to it. The bulls there are of a bigger, more dangerous breed."

Megan watched his face while he talked. His amber eyes were alive with excitement. He had the whitest teeth and the most beautiful mouth she had ever seen. She stared at the cleft in his chin and wondered what it would be like to kiss him there. And because she felt a sudden, pleasant warming, she looked down at the hands that moved so expressively when he talked. They were fine hands with long, delicate fingers. She thought of them holding a sword and asked, "Why do you do it? Why do you fight bulls?"

His dark brows came together in a frown. "It's what I do. It's who I am."

"Who you are?" Megan shook her head. "I don't understand."

"It's what I was brought up to be. The art of *tauromaquia*, of bullfighting, is a tradition in my family. My grandfather was a matador, as was his father before him. The first Montoyas came here from Spain in 1700 and built the house we live in. When my grandfather married my grandmother, their ranches were joined, and today my family has one of the largest brave bull ranches in Mexico."

"Was your father a matador, too?"

"Of course." Ricardo picked up his glass of wine. "He was one of the best and on the way to the top when he received the goring that almost killed him. It happened in a small town where there was no hospital or competent doctor, and he almost died. It took him a year to recover, and after that he was never able to fight again. Now he's my manager. He takes care of everything for me. I couldn't get along without him."

"But if he was so badly hurt...I mean, if he knows how dangerous it is, I would think he'd be afraid to have you doing what he did."

"No, no, no. He watches out for me so that what happened to him will never happen to me."

Megan thought about the young bulls and the cows with their razor-sharp horns that Ricardo had tested the day before. Ricardo, not his father. She didn't say anything else because she didn't want to spoil this perfect evening, but she was suddenly aware of how different she and Ricardo were, and that when the summer was over, she would go back to school and he would go to Spain. While she was occupied with textbooks and lecture halls he would be fighting bulls.

He asked her questions about herself and her family. "I can't understand why they allowed you to come to Mexico alone. Isabel is twenty-six and she still lives at home. It isn't proper for a single woman, no matter what her age is, to live alone or to travel alone."

"Rubbish!"

His eyebrows shot up. "I beg your pardon?"

"That's old-fashioned rubbish. Women today aren't little hothouse flowers, Ricardo. I'm quite capable of taking care of myself, whether I'm in Miami or Mexico."

"Are you?" For a long moment she didn't speak; he only looked at her, the slightest of smiles curving his lips. Then he pushed his chair back and said, "Come and dance with me."

The guitarist began to sing "Strangers in the Night" in Spanish. Ricardo cupped her hand and brought it up against his chest, and she felt ... enfolded by him. And when he brushed his lips against the top of her head and murmured, "While you're here *I* will take care of you, little *gringa,*" she felt her knees weaken.

They didn't speak as they danced in the shadows, her head against his shoulder, the warmth of his body so close to hers. Other couples drifted away. The candles burned low, flickered and died. And still they danced, alone in the moonlight, with only the sweet, sad music of the guitar.

It was late when he took her back to the Chavez house. He escorted her to the gate and, hesitating there, he asked, "What time are you out of school tomorrow?"

"At one."

"I'll pick you up and we'll have lunch. Yes?"

Megan took a deep breath of the jasmine-scented night. "Yes." Then she waited for him to kiss her.

But he didn't. Instead he took her hand and brought it to his lips. "Good night, little *gringa,*" he murmured. "Sleep with the angels."

But it was a long time before Megan was able to sleep. She lay in bed, thinking about the night and the music, and how she had felt in his arms.

She awoke just before dawn to the sound of music. Sure that she was dreaming, she snuggled back down under the blanket. But the music kept playing and finally she realized it wasn't a dream; there really was music, and it was just below her window.

She got up, put her robe on, walked barefoot to the French doors of her room and stepped out onto the balcony. The group of mariachis below in the patio began to play "Strangers in the Night." Ricardo smiled up at her, bowed and doffed his sombrero.

"What are you doing?" Megan whispered down at him. "You'll wake everyone in the family."

"We're already awake," little Clemente called out from his window.

"Is that your *novio,* your boyfriend?" Juanita asked from her balcony. "Oh, Señorita Megan, how romantic!"

"Lovers at first sight..." the mariachis sang.

Megan pulled the robe closer around her and tried to make her expression severe. But it wasn't any good. In spite of herself she smiled because this was absolutely the most romantic thing that had ever happened to her. She wasn't sure how long she should stand here, or if she should even be out on her balcony at all. Maybe it wasn't proper. Maybe she should go in and close the French doors.

But, oh, the night was warm and a half-moon shone down, and Ricardo was so handsome standing there below her balcony, singing along with the mariachis as he gazed up at her.

"Señorita Megan?" Señora Chavez, with a shawl over her shoulders, stood in the shadows just inside the balcony and beckoned to her. "It really isn't proper of you to stand outside so long," she whispered.

"But—"

"Just nod to the gentleman and come in."

Megan looked down into the patio. For a moment her gaze met Ricardo's, then she nodded, and with a small lift of her hand, stepped back and closed the French doors.

"That's Ricardo Montoya, isn't it?" the señora asked.

"Yes," Megan whispered.

"He's a fine young man from a good family, but his father..." Señora Chavez looked troubled.

"His father?"

"He wouldn't approve, not at this point in Ricardo's career."

"Approve?" Megan was puzzled. "Of what? Of Ricardo serenading me?"

"My dear..." Señora Chavez shook her head. "Young men in Mexico don't serenade a young lady unless they're serious about her."

"Serious?" Megan gulped. "But we've only just met. This was our first date. Ricardo isn't—"

"My husband proposed to me on our first date." Señora Chavez rested her hand on Megan's arm. "Go back to bed, my dear. We'll talk again if you want to."

Megan stood in the middle of the room, alone, listening to the music below. With a sigh she went to the curtained windows and looked down at the moonlit patio.

And it seemed to her as she stood there that she could hear the beating of her heart. And his.

It had been so long ago, yet, as she sat here beside him, time faded away. There was only the two of them, together now without bitterness or rancor. He moaned and asked, "Meggie? Where's Meggie?"

"I'm here, darling," she whispered. "I'm here, Ricardo."

His eyelids flickered for a moment, but he didn't respond.

Another doctor and a nurse came. The doctor asked Megan to leave while he examined Ricardo, but she shook her head and, moving out of his way, stood in a corner and watched him pull back the sheet and blanket.

The doctor removed the bandage on the right side of Ricardo's stomach. Megan bit down hard on her lower lip. The jagged wound ran from his groin almost to his hip, angry red against his golden skin. The nurse handed the doctor a solution, and he dabbed it on the wound. The muscles on Ricardo's stomach contracted, and he moaned low in his throat.

The nurse put a fresh bandage on, and before she could cover Ricardo again the doctor ran his knuckle down Ricardo's right foot. When there was no response, he did the same to the left foot. Again there was no response. He shook his head and said, "Cover him," to the nurse.

"What is it?" Megan asked. "What's the matter?"

"Are you a relative?"

"I'm his wife."

"His condition is grave, *señora*."

Megan waited.

"If he survives the next twenty-four hours, I believe he'll recover. But there's a problem with his back. In my opinion surgery is necessary. It's risky of course, but if it isn't done, I'm afraid Ricardo will have great difficulty walking, if indeed he'll ever walk at all."

The doctor took his glasses off and pinched the skin between his eyebrows. "Señor Montoya has said he won't allow his son to take the risk. You're Ricardo's wife. Perhaps you could talk to Señor Montoya—"

"Talk to me about what?"

Franco Montoya stood in the doorway of his son's room, his face white with anger, his fists clenched as though to strike. He was a forceful-looking man, not as tall as Ricardo, but of a stronger, sturdier build. His hair was gray, he had a full mustache and his eyes were like cold gray steel.

"What are you doing here?" he demanded.

"I've come to see Ricardo," Megan said.

"He doesn't want to see you."

"Franco, please..." Josefa Montoya, a small woman with warm brown eyes and a lined but kindly face, put a hand on her husband's arm.

He shrugged it off. "This woman hasn't any right to be here," he said to the doctor. "I don't want her anywhere near my son."

"But she said she was his wife, Señor Montoya."

"His *ex*-wife."

Megan shook her head. "No, Franco. Ricardo and I are separated, but I'm still his wife." She forced a tight, angry smile. "Don't you remember? You were the one who objected to a divorce because of the church. I wanted it, but you talked Ricardo into getting a legal separation instead."

"You have no right—"

"Franco, please." Josefa stepped around in front of her husband and took Megan's hands in hers. "I'm glad you've come. Ricardo will be, too, when he..."

She began to cry, and Megan put her arms around her.

"I want you out of here," Franco said in a voice shaking with anger.

"And I want all of you out in the hall this minute!" The doctor, his voice as angry as Franco's, opened the door. "I won't stand for this kind of commotion in my patient's room. Out!"

Franco shot him an angry glance, but he strode through the door. Megan, her arm around Josefa, followed.

"What just happened in there won't happen again," the doctor said. "If it does, I'll leave orders that no one is to be admitted to the room. Is that clear?"

"Yes." Josefa glared at her husband. "It is perfectly clear. We'll work out a schedule of visits." To Megan she said, "You look tired, my dear. Why don't you go back to Isabel's and get some rest?"

"Isabel's? Isabel's?" Franco's face was mottled with rage.

"She called Megan last night," his wife said. "And I'm glad she did." She took Megan's hand again. "We'll stay with Ricardo tonight. You stay with him tomorrow. How's that?"

Megan didn't want to leave, but she knew Josefa was trying to be fair and that she had to compromise.

"All right." She kissed Josefa's cheek. "But you'll call me if there's any change."

"Of course, I will."

Megan started to turn away but stopped and looked back at Franco. "You got rid of me once. Know that you won't get rid of me this time. I'm going to stay until I know Ricardo is out of danger." She lifted her chin. "And for as long after that as he needs me."

"Meggie? Meggie? Where are you? Where...?"

Was it only a dream, or had he really heard her voice?

"Meggie?" he said again, his voice as weak and mewling as a kitten's. But she didn't answer.

He fought to open his eyes, but they were too heavy. He had to sleep. Had to...

He dreamed she was here with him, that she held his hand and told him everything would be all right and that she would never leave him.

He dreamed . . .

Of the afternoon he had picked her up from school after their first date. She was wearing a pink dress that fitted tightly around her waist and flared to her knees. Her pale blond hair was loose around her shoulders, and her eyes were as blue as the sky.

He drove out of town, up into the hills. "We're going to a special place for lunch," he told her.

She turned and smiled at him. The wind blew her marvelous hair back from her face, and he thought he had never seen anyone as beautiful as she was.

He had known from the moment that Isabel had introduced them that there was something special about this little *gringa* whose smile illuminated her face. She had a sprinkling of freckles across her nose and cheeks, and an infinitely kissable mouth. She was a delicate butterfly of a girl, and he had made up his mind he wanted to know her better.

He hadn't kissed her last night, but he would today.

When he turned off the road onto a dirt path, she looked at him questioningly but didn't say anything. He drove until he reached a grove of leafy green pepper trees and parked. Helping Megan out of the car, he took out the picnic basket with the lunch his mother had fixed.

"It's beautiful here," she said, and looked around with the eyes of a child who had just received a wonderful gift.

He wanted to kiss her then, but he didn't.

He spread a blanket under the trees, and she opened the picnic basket. There was cold chicken and small ham sandwiches, ripe red tomatoes, tangerines, thick slices of chocolate cake and a thermos of lemonade.

After they ate, they lay on their backs and looked up at the clouds.

"Look," he said, pointing upward, "there's a pasture filled with brave bulls. See? There, right at the point of the mountains."

But Megan shook her head. "I see little girls in white summer dresses." She turned and looked at him. "We're very different."

"I know," he said, and kissed her.

Her lips were soft and sweetly innocent. He wanted to touch her breasts, but he didn't because he was afraid she would be frightened and move away. Instead he whispered her name against her lips. "Meggie. Oh, Meggie."

"I'm here," she said.

He opened his eyes. "Meggie?"

She touched the side of his face. "Yes, Ricardo."

"What ... what happened? I dreamed you ..." He tried to sit up, but when he couldn't, he fell back against the pillows and grimaced in pain. "I was hurt. Sunday. Yesterday?"

Megan shook her head. "Two days ago."

"You came from Florida?"

"Of course, I came, as soon as Isabel called me."

Dark eyes, pain-filled and questioning, looked up at her. "It's been a long time."

"Yes."

"You haven't changed."

"Yes, I have." She touched the scar at the side of his mouth. "This is new."

"I got it two years ago." He closed his eyes. "Why did you come, Megan?"

Megan. Not Meggie.

"Because you were hurt," she said. "Pilar is here, too, Ricardo. She's staying with Isabel. She wants to see you."

"Not when I'm like this."

"In a few days, when you're better."

"How is she?"

"She's beautiful, Ricardo. You're going to be so proud of her."

"It's been so long."

Megan felt the tears start to fall. "I know."

He reached for her hand. "Don't leave me, Meggie."

"I won't."

"I'm tired."

"Sleep then. I'll be here when you awaken."

He felt the brush of her lips against his forehead. It's only a dream, he told himself. She'll be gone when I open my eyes.

He slept again, and dreamed again, and when he opened his eyes, the doctor and a nurse were bending over him.

"We're going to change your bandage now, Señor Montoya," the doctor said. "Then we'll talk. Your wife may stay if she wishes."

His wife. He turned his head and saw her sitting on the other side of the bed. "It's all right if you want to wait in the hall," he told her.

But she shook her head and stayed beside him and held his hand while the doctor probed and cleaned the wound. Sweat beaded Ricardo's brow, but he didn't speak or move until the doctor finished and the nurse put a fresh bandage on.

"There's a problem with your legs, Matador," the doctor said. He pulled back the sheet that covered Ricardo and, blocking Ricardo's view, scraped a fingernail down the right foot. "Do you feel that?"

Ricardo tightened his grip on Megan's hand. "What? No, I don't feel anything. What's wrong with my legs?"

The doctor covered him. "When the bull caught you, you were slammed hard against the *barrera*. The blow injured your back." He took his glasses off and rubbed his eyes. "There's pressure on your spine. I believe surgery will relieve it, but there's a risk, of course. Your father's against it. I can understand his concern, but without the surgery..." He hesitated. "Without it I'm afraid you'll never walk properly again, if at all."

Ricardo's grip on Megan's hand was painful, but she didn't pull away.

"I'll have the surgery," he said.

The doctor nodded. "I'll have Dr. Cartas come in and speak to you. He's a neurosurgeon, one of the best. If you continue to recover, I'd say we could schedule the surgery for early next week."

"Thank you, Doctor."

Ricardo was silent when the doctor left.

"Would you like a glass of water?" Megan asked.

"Yes, please."

She helped him to raise his head and held a straw to his lips. After he took a few sips, she wet a cloth and wiped off his face. "Better?"

"Better." He looked up at her. "I want to have the surgery, Meggie."

"I know."

"Will you stay until I have it? Until I know..."

She covered his hand with hers. "Of course, I'll stay."

"I know you have the business, the motel. I don't want it to be difficult for you."

"It won't be. I have a manager. Her name is Agnes Zeller. She's a prim and proper spinster lady in her early fifties, a formidable woman, and I trust her completely. She'll take care of everything while Pilar and I are away."

"I want to see Pilar." He rubbed his thumb across the back of Megan's hand. "Does she look like you?"

"She looks like both of us." Megan smiled. "She has your eyes." She touched the cleft in his chin. "And this."

"Will you bring her tomorrow?"

"Yes, Ricardo."

His eyes drifted closed. "Tell me...tell me about our daughter, Meggie."

"She's a wonderful child, Ricardo. She's bright and happy and nice, and sometimes she's as stubborn as a mule."

He smiled, and some of the tension went out of his face.

"I'm not sure whether she gets that from you or from me," Megan went on. "Maybe from both of us. She does well in school. She loves to fish, and last year she won a prize for catching the biggest bonefish in Key Largo."

So she continued, telling him about the daughter he hadn't seen in five years.

And at last, still clasping her hand, he slept.

Chapter 3

Isabel and her husband, Fernando Garcia, a sturdy, mustachioed man in his early forties, took Pilar out for dinner and a movie that night. But Megan, too emotionally exhausted by everything that had happened the past few days, begged off. She needed time to be alone and sort out her feelings.

There had been times during the past five years—days, even weeks at a time—when she hadn't thought about Ricardo. She had built a new life for herself and her daughter in Florida. She had been busy and reasonably content. She dated occasionally, casual dates with men who were gentlemanly and safe. She had told herself, whenever she allowed herself to think about Ricardo, that she had gotten over him.

She knew now that she hadn't; she'd known when she walked into this hospital room that she still loved him. She wasn't sure what to do about it, or how he felt. He had been glad to see her, but that didn't mean he still loved her, or that he cared or remembered how it had been in the early days when their love was new and there was no bitterness.

Megan lay back on the bed in Isabel's guest room and closed her eyes. She thought of the time gone by and the way it had been . . . eight long years ago.

They saw each other every day for the next two weeks. Ricardo picked her up when school let out at two, and they spent the rest of the day and evening together. They went to dinner, to movies and to concerts. They took day trips out of San Rafael to surrounding towns and archaeological sites. And every night he took her back to the Chavez house it became harder to say good-night.

She loved Ricardo's urgent kisses, loved sitting in the dark closeness of his car and feeling the press of his body so close to hers. She was experiencing all sorts of wonderful new sensations that both frightened and excited her. She wanted him to kiss her and stroke her breasts forever, and she couldn't understand why sometimes he got angry and pushed her away from him.

"Go in the house," he would say in a choked, no-nonsense voice. "Right now, Megan!" And he would open the car door and all but push her toward the Chavez house. But the next night it would be the same again: the urgent kisses, the gentle touching.

One late afternoon they drove out to the place where they had picnicked two weeks before. They walked hand in hand through fields of bright orange poppies, columbine and wild daisies. And though the day was bright with promise and she loved being there with

Ricardo, Megan felt a sudden sadness because the summer had to end, because they both had to go away.

"You'll be leaving soon," she said.

He stopped and looked at her. "Yes."

"I envy you. Going to Spain, I mean."

"Come with me."

"Sure." She turned away.

"You could come later. Maybe for Christmas."

Megan shook her head. "I always spend Christmas with my folks. Besides, I couldn't afford a trip like that. Neither could they."

"I'll be back in Mexico next summer. You'll come back then."

"Maybe."

And because she wouldn't look at him, he put a finger under her chin and raised her face to his. "I'll miss you, Meggie," he said. "You can't know how much I'll miss you."

"Ricardo, I—"

He stopped her words with a kiss, and she kissed him back with fervor and desperation because they were going to leave each other, and though he had said they would see each other next year, she knew they wouldn't. He might still be in Spain. She would be graduating and looking for a job. This one brief summer was all they were ever going to have.

All of the feelings they had held in check for the past two weeks rushed to the surface. Ricardo tightened his arms around her and she moved closer. "You know how much I want you," he murmured against her lips.

She pressed her body to his, trembling with the same wanting need, and when he sank down into the field of orange poppies, she clung to him.

He cupped her breasts, and she moaned into his mouth. *"Querida,"* he said against her lips. "My Meggie, *mi muñaquita,* my little doll."

They lay back on the sun-warmed earth. He trailed kisses across her face, her shoulders. He feathered kisses across her breasts. And when he took a nipple to lap and tease, she became incoherent with pleasure. And though she said, "We've got to stop, we mustn't do this," she made no move away until he raised her skirt and touched her between her legs.

She grasped his hand to stop him then, but he said, "No, Meggie. Let me touch you here." And when he pulled her panties down and cupped her there, her body stiffened, but she didn't move away.

"So soft," he said as he caressed her. "So moist and ready." He began to kiss her breasts again, and all the while his fingers teased, teased until her body heated and she moaned with pleasure.

He stopped and, moving up over her, said, in a voice hoarse with need, "I have to, Meggie. Please. Is it all right? Can I . . . ?"

"Yes," she whispered. "Yes. Ricardo."

He looked down at her, then quickly rolled away and began tugging at his jeans. She didn't look at him, but when he brought his body over hers, she felt his hardness and was afraid.

He kissed her, and against her lips asked, "Is this your first time?"

Hot color flushed her cheeks.

"Tell me," he said.

She nodded.

"Ah, Meggie." He kissed the side of her face. "My sweet girl. I'll be careful, *querida.* I'll try not to hurt you." He grasped her hips then, and as gently as he could, he joined his body to hers.

She cried out and he said, "Shh, it's all right now. I won't hurt you again." And he began to move against her, slowly, deeply, carefully.

The pain faded, and a feeling unlike anything she'd ever known surged through her. She murmured his name and lifted her body to his.

His movements quickened and the breath came hard in his throat. He took her mouth again, and his hands went around her back to bring her even closer.

"Oh!" she whispered. "Oh, stop! Something... something's happening, Ricardo. Wait! Stop!"

But he didn't stop. He moved hard against her, and the breath came fast in his throat. She didn't understand. Sensations she'd never before experienced gripped her. She was spinning out of control, dizzy with an immensity of feeling she'd never known before.

"Yes," he whispered. "Oh, yes!" He kissed her and made her a prisoner of his arms. He held her as if he would never let her go.

Suddenly it was as though her body merged with his. She was a part of him, and she cried aloud with the wonder of it because she was moving with him, riding to glory with him, past all thought, all restraint.

She cried out, and tried to smother her cry against his shoulder. But he took her mouth again, and he cried out as she had, and his body exploded against hers.

Afterward they lay in each other's arms, there in the field of bright orange poppies. She felt the hot earth against her back and gazed up at a sky that had never been so blue before. Her body felt free and light, one with everything around her. And with Ricardo.

He kissed her ever so gently, her eyelids, her nose, her mouth. He ran his hands up and down her back, lightly caressing her. "My Meggie."

They spoke little on the way back to San Rafael. Now and then Megan stole a glance at Ricardo. He was frowning and looked troubled. When they got to the Chavez house, he kissed her. Then, not quite meeting her eyes, he said, "I'll call you."

Megan cried that night, her face against her pillow so that no one would hear her, because she knew she would never see him again. What had been for her the most important, the most amazing and beautiful thing that had ever happened in all her twenty-one years, hadn't meant anything to him. He was going away. He would forget her.

The next morning there were dark circles under her eyes, and when Señora Chavez asked her if she was all right, the tears started again.

"I'm ... I'm just homesick," she managed to say.

She did her best to eat, but only succeeded in drinking half a cup of hot chocolate and eating a small piece of toasted *bolillo* before she went to school.

She told herself that Ricardo would be waiting for her when school finished. Every few minutes she glanced at her watch, and when finally two o'clock came, she picked up her Spanish text and notebook and headed for the door.

Isabel stopped her. "Wait a moment." When the other students filed out, she asked, "What is it, Megan? Is something the matter? Is it Ricardo?"

Megan looked at her, then quickly away.

"Don't break your heart over him," Isabel said gently. "He's going away and he'll be gone for a year." She took Megan's hand. "You're very different people, Megan. Your backgrounds, your cultures are so different."

Megan swiped at the tears that rolled down her cheeks. "I know."

Another day went by. And another.

On the evening of the fourth day he came to the Chavez home. She was in her room trying to study when Señora Chavez came to her door and announced, "Ricardo Montoya is here. He would like to speak to you."

Megan started to shake. "Tell him...tell him I'll be there in a moment," she managed to say.

She brushed her hair and changed her blouse. She tried to pinch color into her too-pale cheeks. She took deep breaths because somebody had once told her that helped when you were scared and nervous and your knees were shaking and the palms of your hands were damp. She wiped them on her skirt, then brushed her hair again.

He was talking to Señor and Señora Chavez when she came into the *sala*. He stood and said, *"Buenas noches, Megan. ¿Cómo estás?"*

"Bien, gracias."

"I wonder if you'd like to come out for a little while?"

Megan hesitated for a moment before she nodded. To Señora Chavez she said, "I won't be late, *señora*."

Ricardo took her arm and helped her into the car. "Where are we going?" she asked.

"To the ranch. You met my mother at the *tienta*, but I'd like you to meet her again, when there aren't other people around, I mean."

She looked at him, puzzled. "Why?"

He stopped the car and took a deep breath, and she knew he was as nervous as she was. "Because I want you to marry me."

"Marry...?"

Tears filled her eyes again, and he said, "Don't cry, Meggie. Please, *querida*, don't cry."

"I thought I'd never see you again. I thought because I...because we...we did what we did you didn't want to see me anymore. I thought—"

Ricardo drew her into his arms. "I love you," he said against her hair. "I want to be married to you, Meggie. I want you to come to Spain with me." He kissed her salty lips and licked the tears from her cheeks. "I know it's soon," he said, holding her away from him so that he could look at her. "But I don't want to wait. I want to get married now. Tonight. Tomorrow. Just as soon as we can have the blood tests done and find a judge."

"I...I don't know what to say."

"Say yes." He pulled her across his lap and, cradling her in his arms, he kissed her, kissed her until she was beyond all thought, all will. "Tell me you love me," he said against her lips. "Tell me."

"I love you."

"Say you'll marry me."

She touched his face. "Yes. I'll marry you."

He held her without speaking for a little while, and then he started the car and drove out to the ranch so that he could tell his mother their news.

They were married by a judge four days later. Isabel and his mother were there. And Megan's parents, still in a state of shock at her news, flew in from Miami.

After the wedding, Megan and Ricardo flew to Acapulco for ten heavenly days of sunning and swimming. And lovemaking.

Megan had never known this kind of happiness, this sense of total belonging. She hadn't known it was possible to love anyone as much as she loved Ricardo.

"We'll be like this forever," he said. "You belong to me now."

"Yes, Ricardo. I'm yours, darling. Forever."

Forever lasted for three short years.

They hesitated in the doorway of his hospital room, mother and daughter, holding each other's hand.

Megan, her pale hair brushed back from her face, was conservatively dressed in a gray wool suit and a white silk blouse.

Their daughter, a small, solemn child with blond hair like her mother's, but with her father's eyes, and yes, the same cleft in her small chin, wore a navy blue pleated skirt and a bright red sweater. Her cheeks were pink, her eyes large and questioning as she looked at him.

She cleared her throat and said, *"Hola, Papá. ¿Cómo está?"*

"You speak Spanish." That pleased him.

"Sí. Well, a little."

He motioned her forward, and she came to the side of his bed, leaned down and brushed a kiss against his cheek. Then she blushed and backed away.

"How are you feeling this morning?" Megan asked him.

"Better. I saw the neurosurgeon. He's scheduled my surgery for next Monday. Will you still be here?"

"Of course. We both will."

"What about Pilar's school?"

"She brought her class assignments with her. In two weeks school will be out for Christmas vacation and she'll have another two weeks. You'll be well by then."

And you will leave, he thought.

"Have you spoken to your father?" she asked. "About the surgery?"

"Yes. He doesn't want me to have it." He looked up at her. "He thinks I'm making a mistake. Do you?"

"No, I don't, Ricardo. I think you're right to want to do it."

"Thank you, Megan. It helps to know you feel as I do."

She nodded, then glanced at Pilar and said, "I haven't had lunch yet. I'm going to go downstairs and have something to eat while the two of you visit."

Pilar shot her a worried glance, but Megan smiled, and with a wave of her hand went out and closed the door behind her.

When they were alone, Ricardo said, "Your mother told me you won a fishing prize for bonefishing. I've been deep-sea fishing, but I don't even know what a bonefish is."

Pilar moved a chair closer to the bed and sat down. "I went deep-sea fishing once. I hooked a great big fish, but he got away from me." She grinned. "Probably because he weighed about a hundred pounds more than I do. But bonefishing is different. They only weigh four or five pounds, but they're really tough. I mean, they fight and you have to work hard to pull them in."

"It sounds like fun. I'd like to try it sometime."

"Maybe if you ever come to Florida we could go."

"I'd like that."

"How come you never did? Come to Florida, I mean."

"Well, I..." Ricardo began, trying to think of what to say.

But before he could say anything Pilar asked, in a voice so low that he could barely hear her, "Why don't you like us?"

He felt as though he'd received a blow to his mid-section. For a moment he couldn't even speak. "I do like you, Pilar. Both you and your mother mean a great deal to me. I love you."

She shook her head and kept her eyes lowered so that she wouldn't have to look at him. "You never come to see us or ask me to come and visit you." She folded the pleats of her blue skirt. "Was it because I did something bad? Is that why you don't like me?"

He felt as though his heart had been torn in two. "No. Oh, *querida,* no." He reached for her hand. "I've loved you from the day you were born, Pilar. From the very first moment I held you in my arms."

"Then why...?" She shook her head. "I don't understand," she murmured.

Ricardo closed his eyes and prayed for the right words to take away the doubt and sadness from the sweet face of his child. "When your mother and I decided to live apart, we thought it would be better for you not to have divided loyalties. Do you understand?"

Pilar shook her head. "I've got some friends whose parents are divorced. They spend part of the time with their mothers and part of the time with their fathers. Sometimes they're sad when they go and sad when they come back, but that's because both parents want them."

"I wanted you, Pilar. Believe me, I wanted you." Words didn't come easily, and he wondered as he had so many times before if he and Megan had been wrong all of these years in thinking they were doing what was best for Pilar.

"We didn't want you to have to divide your loyalty between your mother and me," he said. "We thought we were doing what was best for you, but we were wrong. I'm sorry I haven't been there for you, Pilar, but I will be from now on. That's a promise."

She looked at him, her wide, dark eyes serious, troubled. "Why did you and Mom . . . ? You know."

"Separate?" Ricardo shifted into a more comfortable position. "I suppose it was because of the bulls, because it made her afraid when I fought. She couldn't understand why I did it and I couldn't understand why she couldn't understand." He squeezed her hand. "Sometimes grown-ups can be pretty complicated."

Pilar sighed and nodded in agreement. "I know." She touched the cleft in his chin. "We're sorta alike."

He thought his heart would break with loving her, but he made himself smile and say, "More than sorta."

And he remembered the day Megan had told him she was pregnant.

He'd held her away from him. *"¡Embarazada!"* he'd cried. *"¿Verdaderamente?* Are you sure? Is everything all right?"

"Yes," she'd said with a laugh. "Everything's fine. I've never been healthier."

And it was true. Megan had bloomed. She'd had a healthy nine months, but when the time came for the baby to be born, she'd had a hard time.

In those days in Mexico the man wasn't allowed into the delivery room, but he had insisted. "She's my wife," he'd said. "She's in a foreign country and this is her first baby. I want to be with her."

He'd held her hand and said, "That's it, Meggie. You're doing fine, *querida*. Hold on, Meggie. Hold on." And at last their daughter had been born.

"But you wanted a boy," Meggie had said when she held the baby to her breast. "Are you sure you aren't disappointed?"

"Disappointed?" He had picked Pilar up. She was so unbelievably tiny, so incredibly fragile. He'd brushed her cheek with his fingertip and whispered, "She's so beautiful. And we made her with our love, Meggie. She's perfect and she's a part of us."

He knew now how wrong he had been all these years to turn his back on Pilar, and to tell himself that he had been doing it for her own good. He'd been wrong, terribly wrong, and he vowed he would make it up to her, that he would be the father he hadn't been for the past five years.

"How would you like to come and visit me at the ranch next summer?" he asked.

Her face lighted up in a smile. "I'd love it! What about Mom? Can she come, too?"

"If she wants to," Ricardo said carefully.

"If she wants to what?" Megan asked from the doorway.

"Come and visit Dad next summer," Pilar said, her eyes glowing with pleasure. "Dad said I could, Mom. Will it be okay? Can I do it?"

"Of course, you can, sweetheart."

"Will you come?"

Megan looked at Ricardo, then away. "I'm going to have the motel painted next summer, Pilar, so I'll need to be there." She rested a hand on her daughter's pale hair. "But you can go, sweetie. The ranch is a beautiful place. You'll love it."

Pilar turned to hug her and said, "Thanks, Mom."

And over their daughter's head Ricardo whispered, "Thank you, Meggie."

They left a little while later because it was almost time for his father and mother to arrive. Pilar kissed him good-bye, but not quite as shyly as she had kissed him when she arrived. He hugged her hard and said, "I'll see you tomorrow, *muchachita.*"

Pilar grinned. "I like that. It means little girl, doesn't it?"

"Yes, and you're my little girl. *¿Sí?*"

"Yes. *Sí.*" She kissed him again, and to her mother she said, "Your turn."

Megan froze, embarrassed, not quite sure what to say or do. But before she could say anything Ricardo lifted his arms. "For old time's sake," he said. Megan took a step forward. He put his arms around her, and their lips met, gently, barely touching. "Meggie," he whispered so softly that only she could hear.

When she straightened, tears misted her eyes, and she brushed them away before Pilar could see them. "We ... we'll see you tomorrow." She placed a hand on Ricardo's shoulder. "Sleep well."

"With the angels," he answered.

It was happening all over again, and he didn't want it to. Meggie had left him because she hadn't had courage or love enough to face the kind of life he lived, or to accept him as the man he was. She had gone away and had taken his child from him. He didn't think he could ever forgive her for that.

Now she was here and he wasn't sure why. Had she come because she still cared about him, or because of some innate sense of it being the right thing to do?

She was even more beautiful than he remembered. When she left him, she had been in her early twenties. She was older now, more poised than she had been. Her body was richer, riper. Her breasts were larger than he remembered, her...

Suddenly, unbidden, his body tightened with need. He balled his hands into fists and cursed aloud. "Damn you!" he muttered. "Damn you, Megan, for making me want you again!"

There had been other women since she had walked out of his life. With one or two of them he had thought, Yes, this would be good. I need someone. I could be happy with this woman. But each time thoughts of Meggie and of how it had been for them had held him back.

Now she was here, and all of the old memories had come flooding back, memories of the girl she had been, of their first kiss, of the first time they had made love.

"Meggie," he whispered. Why had she come back?

Chapter 4

Megan arrived at the hospital early on the morning that Ricardo was to have surgery. Isabel had come with her, and when they reached Ricardo's room she said, "Father is probably with him. Would you like me to go in first? To make sure it's all right?"

Megan shook her head. "I'm not the timid girl I was when Ricardo and I married, Isabel. Your father doesn't scare me now."

Isabel smiled. *"Muy bien, amiga.* After you."

They went in together. Franco, who sat on one side of Ricardo's bed, looked up when he saw the two women and scowled.

"Buenos... buenos días," Ricardo said groggily. "They gave me a shot a while ago. I'm a little... out of it."

"He shouldn't be disturbed," Franco said.

"I'm not going to disturb him." Megan moved closer to the bed. "Pilar wanted to send you something, Ricardo." She handed him a tissue-wrapped box. "Shall I open it for you?"

"Yes . . . please."

She unwrapped the paper, opened the box and handed it to him. Inside was a six-inch silver fish on top of a plaque that read: Winner, Junior Bonefish Competition. Pilar Montoya, September 15, 1990.

"Pilar wanted you to have it," Megan said. "She said to tell you that when you come to Florida she'll teach you all about bonefishing."

He looked at the silver fish through eyes made bleary by the injection. "Tell her . . . it's the nicest present anyone has ever given me." He looked up at Megan. "Except when you gave me her."

Megan swallowed hard. "I'll tell her," she whispered.

Two orderlies came in with a gurney. "It's time, Matador," one of them said.

Ricardo looked at his father. "Don't worry," he murmured. "It's going to be all right."

"You know I object to this whole procedure," Franco said. "You'd never have gone ahead with it if it hadn't been for her."

Ricardo shook his head. "The decision was mine, Father. Please . . . wish me luck."

Franco's face tightened. *"Suerte,"* he said, and walked out of the room.

Megan took Ricardo's hand. "It's going to be all right, Ricardo. You're going to be fine."

His eyelids were so heavy that he could barely keep them open. He felt the touch of her lips against his forehead, the press of her hand on his.

"Sleep with the angels," she whispered.

* * *

"How do you feel?" Dr. Cartas asked when they put him on the table.

"Drunk."

"Splendid." Cartas chuckled. He nodded to a nurse, and something jabbed into Ricardo's arm.

"Count backward," Dr. Cartas said. *"Cien..."*

"Cien, noventa y nueve, noventa y ocho, noventa..."

Darkness... through the darkness, dreams, pictures in his mind, flashes of memory. Vivid... real.

Meggie, half-covered with soapy bubbles, laughing up at him from the big old-fashioned tub with the claw feet. Reaching her hand out. "The water's fine. Join me."

Morning sun turning her skin to gold. Rise of breast, peach-pink nipples, tender curves and hollows, precious secret places his lips had touched.

A golden Spanish afternoon... making love to Meggie in a field of yellow daisies... murmured whispers of, "Yes, oh, yes."

Meggie... in daylight, in shadow...

Meggie.

Pain.

His mother said, *"Mi hijo,* my son." And he opened his eyes.

"It's all right, Mama," he murmured. "Where's Meggie?"

"I'm here, Ricardo."

"Fish."

"What?"

"Want to hold it."

She put the small trophy in his hand.

"Yes," he whispered, and closed his eyes.

He opened them again, later, when the doctor came in. "You're doing fine," Cartas said. "Let's have a look at your legs."

Cartas pulled back the sheet, took a pencil from the pocket of his white coat and ran it down the middle of Ricardo's right foot. There was no response. He ran it down the left foot. Again there was no response, no flicker of movement.

"Well…" Cartas's expression was difficult to read. "It's early yet, Matador. Give it time."

Time. Ricardo closed his eyes so that they wouldn't see his fear.

When he awoke again, it was night. In the dim light beside his bed he saw Meggie. "Have you been here all the time?" he asked.

"Yes. How do you feel?"

"Thirsty. May I have a glass of water?"

"Of course." She poured a glass from the pitcher next to his bed, lifted his head and held the glass to his lips.

"What time is it?"

"Almost three."

"You should rest. I'm all right. You don't need to stay."

"I want to."

He pushed the sheet and the blanket away from his chest. "So warm."

Megan touched his forehead. "You'll feel better if I sponge you off." She went into the bathroom and poured cool water into a basin. Then, taking a wash-cloth from under his nightstand, she wet it and began to bathe his face.

"Good," he murmured. "Feels good."

She bathed his arms and, pulling away the sheet that covered his legs, began to wipe first one, then the other with the damp cloth. When she touched his right foot with it, his toes curled.

"Too cold," he said. "It . . . Meggie! Meggie, I can feel it!"

Her hands began to shake. She put the wet cloth against his other foot. The toes curled.

"Sweet Jesus," Ricardo whispered. "I can feel it."

Water spilled over the edge of the basin. Megan put it down and grasped the rails at the foot of the bed.

He wiggled his toes again and looked at her. His eyes, wide with wonder and relief, met hers. "I can move them, Meggie. I can feel again."

Two days later a nurse and an orderly helped Ricardo walk up and down the corridor outside his room. He was still weak and he walked slowly, but the important thing was that he walked.

"You're a damn good patient and I'm a damn good doctor," Cartas said. "Another week and you'll be ready to go back to the ranch. But I want you to rest for at least four months, Ricardo. Five would be better."

"Five months!" Ricardo looked outraged. "I have to train. I have to—"

"You have to take care of yourself," the doctor barked. "The operation was successful and your legs are getting stronger, but the goring to your stomach was one of the worst I've ever seen. It's a miracle you survived."

He rested a hand on Ricardo's shoulder. "It's going to take you a long time to heal, Matador, and to

get the strength back in your legs. You've got to take
it easy if you ever hope to fight again.''

If he ever hoped to fight again! *Por Dios,* it was his
life. It was a part of him, in his blood, as holy to him
as the church. He would never give it up. He had sac-
rificed too much.

It had cost him his wife and daughter.

It was strange, he thought. Meggie hadn't minded
his fighting in the early months of their marriage.
She'd loved the color and the pageantry of the corrida, the excitement. It was only later that she
changed. . . .

They left for Spain right after their Acapulco honeymoon. They bought a small Spanish car, big enough
for the two of them, for their luggage, his *espuerta,* the
bag for his cape and muleta, and the *fundón* with the
set of his swords.

He fought almost every Sunday that season, trav-
eling from city to city with Meggie beside him—to
Cordoba, Granada, Valencia, Málaga, Sevilla and
Madrid. She attended every corrida, sitting in a ring-
side *barrera,* cheering him on, happy to be the wife of
the Mexican matador that the proud Spanish people
had taken to their hearts.

She loved Spain; they loved each other.

Each morning he awakened her with tender kisses
and soft caresses. Half-asleep, she would turn to him,
nuzzling sweet and warm against his throat, opening
her arms to hold him close.

Never before or since would he be so completely one
with another.

But everything changed after Madrid.

The day was bright and filled with promise. He had fought in the Plaza Monumental de las Ventas the week before to a sellout crowd. By Thursday all of the tickets to the coming Sunday fight, which was to be a *mano a mano,* a two-man corrida with Spain's number one matador of the day, Alesio Rodriguez, were gone and scalpers were getting a hundred dollars for a seat in the gallery.

He and Megan slept late, and when they awakened, they had breakfast in their suite, which overlooked the Plaza de España. At three that afternoon his cuadrilla, the two men he had brought with him from Mexico to help him, arrived. They helped him dress in his suit of lights, and when he was ready, they drove to Las Ventas.

When they arrived, he kissed Megan and said, "See you back at the hotel after the fight, darling."

But he didn't return to the hotel after the fight; he ended up in the hospital.

Everything went exceptionally well with his first two bulls. He received an ear and ovations on the first, two ears on the second. His third bull weighed almost twelve hundred pounds. A Miura, it had wide but crooked horns, and he didn't know until he began fighting that it was blind in one eye. That made it infinitely more dangerous than a bull with good sight.

"Careful, Matador," Juan Serrano whispered just before he stepped into the rig. "I don't like the looks of this one."

His cape work was good, but he knew with his first *chicuelina* that Juan was right; this was a dangerous animal. But he was determined to do his best with it because the aficionados, the fans, had paid a lot of money to see him and Alesio fight. He would give them their money's worth.

He did a series of veronicas and ended the series with a media-veronica that got the crowd cheering. Next came the *largo afarolada*. He passed the bull, spinning in after it went past. But it spun back so swiftly that he didn't have time to react, and it caught him. The horn ripped into his thigh from knee to hip.

The banderilleros rushed into the ring. Alesio drew the bull away, and they carried him out of the ring to the infirmary where a doctor was waiting. They cut away his pant leg, the doctor applied pressure packs and he was placed in the waiting ambulance.

"I have to wait for my wife," he said. *"Mi esposa."*

But the doctor said, "There's no time, Matador." And he slammed the doors of the ambulance and shouted, *"¡Con prisa!* Hurry!"

They rushed him into surgery and he awakened hours later to find Megan beside him. Her face was ashen, her eyes swollen from weeping.

"You can't do that anymore," she said.

"I don't plan to." He summoned a grin and reached for her hand. "It looked worse than it was, Meggie. I'll be up and around in a couple of weeks and I'll be able to fight in the feria in Valencia next month."

"No!"

"What?" he asked, honestly puzzled. "What did you say?"

"I said no! No more! You have to give it up. You can't fight, ever again."

"Can't fight? What in hell are you talking about?"

"I don't want you ever . . . *ever* to even set foot in a bullring again. I won't have you hurt like you were today. You can't do it, Ricardo. You just can't."

He bristled with anger. "Don't be silly, Megan. It's what I do."

"It's what you did! But not anymore. I want you to promise me you'll never fight again."

"Of course, I won't promise that."

"You have to."

"I don't have to do anything except fight. It's what I do, Megan. It's who I am. I won't let you or anybody else tell me what I can or cannot do."

They argued often in the weeks that followed. When he recovered, they went to Valencia. He fought in Málaga and Alicante after that. He was gored again in Barcelona, but the wound wasn't as bad as the one he'd received in Madrid, so he recovered quickly.

Megan wouldn't go to watch him fight.

"I'm not going to sit there and watch you kill yourself," she shouted at him. "Commit suicide if you want to, but I won't be there to see it."

Each day she grew thinner, and there were dark smudges of fatigue under her eyes because she couldn't sleep. They rarely made love, and when they did, it was with a sense of urgency, of desperation.

Things were better when they returned to Mexico because it wasn't the season of corridas. Megan wanted them to find a home of their own, but he told her he needed to train, that he had to be there on the ranch with his father. He was aware there was some tension between his father and Megan, but because she and his mother and Isabel got along, he told himself in time his father would come around.

His father had been upset because he and Megan had married so quickly. "The girl's an American. She doesn't understand our ways," his father had said. "She'll hold you back."

"No," he'd answered. "Megan loves me. In time she'll understand about the bullfighting."

He was deliriously happy when she told him she was pregnant. They were both excited about the coming birth of their first child, and things were better between them, especially after Pilar was born. She was a happy, healthy baby. His mother and sister loved and fussed over her, but his father only said, "I had hoped you would have a boy," and paid as little attention to their infant daughter as he could.

Ricardo fought that season in Mexico, but Megan didn't attend any of his fights. At the end of the season he went to Colombia, Venezuela and Peru to fight. She didn't go with him. "Because of the baby," she said. "She's too young to travel."

When he returned to Mexico, she was silent and withdrawn. She asked him if they could get a place of their own. "We'll talk about it when we come back from Spain," he said.

At the end of the season in Mexico he took part in the Estoque de Oro, the golden sword competition between six top matadors to see who would receive the award.

"The Estoque is a coveted trophy," he told Megan. "It would mean a great deal to me if you would come and watch me on Sunday."

Later he wondered if it would have made any difference if she hadn't.

She was seated in the front *barrera* with his sister. When the *partida de plaza,* the entrance of the matadors and their cuadrillas began, he crossed the sand with the other matadors, approached the place of the authorities of the bullfight, then went to where Megan and Isabel were and reached up to spread his *capote de paseo,* the ornately embroidered cape he wore draped over his left shoulder, over the front of their *barrera.*

She smiled down at him, and he thought, It's going to be all right.

But it wasn't.

His was the sixth bull of the day. He waited for it on his knees in front of the *toril,* the door from which the bull would emerge. The animal exploded into the plaza, straight for him, and he passed it with a *cambio afarolado* that brought the crowd to their feet.

He loved this bull. It was the best of his season, and he knew he could do wonderful things with it. And he did, even after the bull caught and tossed him. He landed hard, and the bull surged over him, reaching with its horns, trying to rip and tear at his body while the crowd screamed. But he protected himself, scrambled to his feet and waved his helpers away. Then he did two more lances before he retreated to the side with blood running down his leg.

"I'm all right," he told his father. "Bind it quickly."

They cheered him when he went back into the ring. He finished the fight, and when it was over, he was awarded the Estoque de Oro. He circled the giant plaza with cheers from the crowd ringing in his ears. Men threw him their hats and *botas* of wine, the women their high-heeled shoes and bouquets of roses and carnations. Finally he reached the place where Megan had been. His sister was there, but she wasn't.

That night she said, "I can't stand it anymore, Ricardo. I've tried. I really have. But every time you step into the ring I die a little. I can't live with that kind of fear. I can't wait for someone to come and tell me you've been hurt or killed. I just can't..." She turned away from him, her shoulders slumped, her head bowed. Then her shoulders straightened and she said, "Unless you can tell me you'll give it up, I'll have to go away."

"You ask too much of me."

"If you love me, you'll quit."

"If you love me, you'll accept me the way I am." He gripped her shoulders and forced her to face him. "You knew what I did when you married me, Megan. You liked it then. You were proud of me then."

She closed her eyes. "I didn't know," she whispered. "I only saw the excitement and color. I didn't see the danger. I didn't know."

A week later she took their baby daughter and left. And he felt as though half his life were being ripped away from him.

"I love you," he said that last day. "I love our baby. Please don't do this."

"You know what it will take to make me stay."

He looked at her, and at their baby. Then, without a word, he turned and walked away from her.

His mother had wept. His father had said, "Thank God she's out of your life."

Now she had come back into his life, she and his daughter. And he wasn't sure what he was going to do about that.

Chapter 5

"He's really better?" Pilar asked. "Really, Mom?"

"Absolutely." Megan pulled into the hospital parking lot and stopped. "The doctor said your dad will be ready to leave the hospital by the end of the week."

"Where'll he go then?"

"Back to the ranch to recuperate, honey."

"With Grandma and Grandpa?"

Megan nodded and got out of the car. "He's going to need to rest and take it easy, Pilar. His mother and father will take good care of him."

"How come they don't like me?"

"Your grandmother and grandfather?" Megan looked startled. "They...they like you, sweetie. It's just that..." Megan hesitated, searching for the words to try to explain to Pilar why her grandparents had made no attempt to see her or to invite her to the ranch. She didn't want to say, "Your grandmother would, but very likely your grandfather won't let her because of me.''

"I suppose it's because they've never really had a chance to get to know you, Pilar," she said at last. "I mean, because we live in Florida and they live here."

"But we're in Mexico now and I haven't even seen them."

"We got to the hospital at different times, honey. The ranch is almost an hour-and-a-half drive from here. It's a long trip for them every day. They've probably been so concerned about your dad that they haven't thought about anything else."

They got out of the car. "There's something I forgot to tell Isabel," Megan said. "Why don't you go into the coffee shop and buy you and your dad some ice cream while I make the call?"

She left Pilar at the door of the coffee shop, then turned and went back to the reception desk where the phones were. She dialed Isabel's number, and when Isabel answered, Megan said, "I'd like to ask a favor. Do you think if you invited your mother and dad for dinner tonight they'd come?''

"Mother would. I don't know about Dad. But why, Megan? Is something wrong?"

"It's Pilar. She thinks your mother and father don't want to see her. I thought if she spent a little time with them, she might feel better about it."

"Of course, Megan. I should have thought of it myself. If Dad doesn't want to come, I'll have Fernando go out to the ranch for Mother."

"Thanks," Megan said. "Thanks a lot, Isabel." She put the receiver down, and when Pilar came out of the coffee shop carrying two small cartons of ice cream, she said, "Guess what? Your Aunt Isabel has invited your grandparents to dinner tonight. She's absolutely positive your grandmother will come.''

''What about my grandfather?''

Megan's forehead wrinkled in a frown as she hesitated. ''I'm not sure he'll be able to make it, honey.''

''How come?''

''I guess he's pretty busy at the ranch because he's been spending so much time at the hospital with your dad. There's an awful lot to do, running a ranch the size of El Girasol, Pilar.'' And in an attempt to get her daughter's mind off why she hadn't seen her grandparents, Megan said, ''Girasol means sunflower in Spanish, and there's a whole field of them just as you approach the ranch, wild sunflowers, as big and yellow as the sun. They look as if they're welcoming you.''

''I wish I could see them. Maybe we could go out to the ranch sometime.''

''We'll see, honey. But now that your dad is better we really should be getting back to Key Largo.''

''But—''

''No buts, kiddo. It's time we went home.'' Megan gave a gentle tug on Pilar's long braid and thought how pretty her daughter looked this morning in her short, dark skirt and a fuzzy pink sweater that brought out a rosy tint in her golden skin tone. Her big, dark eyes were a startling contrast to her fair hair. She was a pretty girl; in another ten years she'd be a stunning seventeen. And I'll turn gray worrying about her, Megan thought ruefully, and wished she could keep Pilar young forever.

Ricardo was sitting in a big chair beside the bed when they went into the room. He looked up and smiled. "*Buenos días,* princess," he said. "*Buenos días, Megan.*"

"*Buenos días, Papá.*" Pilar crossed the room and kissed him. "I've got chocolate and strawberry ice cream," she said. "Which one do you want?"

"You choose."

"No, you."

"Strawberry?"

She grinned and looked relieved. "Then I'll eat the chocolate." She saw her trophy on the nightstand next to the bed.

Ricardo followed her gaze. "That was a wonderful present, Pilar. It means a lot to me. I know how special it is to you. If you ever want it back—"

"I won't," she said. "I want you to have it." She took a spoonful of her ice cream. "I'll win another one sometime. Maybe even this year."

"I wish I could be there to see you do it."

"You could if you came to Florida."

"Pilar, I—"

"It's real warm there now. Warmer than here. It'd be good for you. You could sun and swim and do stuff like that. Mom has a really nifty sailboat, so we could go sailing and fishing and . . . and it would be a good place to recup . . . to recuper . . ."

"Recuperate," Ricardo said. "I'm sure it would be, Pilar, but . . ." He looked at Megan, not sure what to say. He didn't want to hurt Pilar, but he didn't want to put Megan in a compromising position. "Maybe sometime," he started to say. "But—"

"The Keys are lovely this time of year," Megan said. "And Pilar's right. It would do you good to relax in the sun and swim and—"

"I couldn't impose on you."

"You wouldn't be imposing. I ... we ... we'd love having you, Ricardo. You could stay in one of the efficiencies or on the boat."

"And he could eat with us, couldn't he, Mom?" Pilar turned to her father, her eyes alight with excitement. "Mom's a terrific cook, Dad. She makes the best hush puppies in the Keys."

"Hush puppies? What's that?" he asked, straight-faced. "Quiet little dogs?"

"Oh, Dad!" Pilar giggled. "It's kind of cornmeal fritter that Mom fixes with fish. They're delish." Her face sobered. "Please come home with us, Daddy. We really want you to."

He didn't think he should, and yet ... He thought of what it would be like to get to know this daughter of his. To spend time with her. And with Megan.

Their eyes met. "It would be nice if you could," Megan said softly.

"I'll take you bonefishing," Pilar said.

Ricardo looked at Megan, then at their daughter. It would be wonderful to be able to spend time with the two of them, but still he hesitated, afraid that if he went, it would begin all over again.

He didn't want it to. It had taken him a long time to get over Megan. For months after she had left him he had told himself that he was glad she had gone, that if she wasn't woman enough to love him in spite of what he did, he didn't want her. But he had wanted her desperately. There had been nights when he'd lain alone in their bed, his body tight and hard with wanting her. And other times, especially during those first few months, when he suddenly thought of something he had to tell her, and he would turn to speak to her, forgetting for a moment that she wasn't there.

There had been a part of him that had wanted to forget his macho pride and go after her. Once he almost had. He had packed a bag and called the airline. "Yes, Miami," he had said into the phone, just as his father had walked into the room.

"Miami? What do you mean you're going to Miami? You're fighting in Guadalajara next week."

"I'm going to Megan," he'd said. "I'm going to bring her back."

"Are you out of your mind?" His father's face had gone tight with disbelief and anger. "Forget her, Ricardo It's over. Let it rest. Megan wasn't any good for you. Believe me, you're better off without her. If she had stayed, she would have ruined your career with her constant harping and her fear. Maybe it wasn't her fault that she didn't understand our ways, but you have to face it, Ricardo, she didn't love you enough to let you do what you were born to do."

She hadn't loved him enough. He didn't think he could ever forgive her for that.

"Dad?" Pilar leaned forward in her chair, her eyes eager, expectant.

She was his child. And yet...

He looked at Megan. Her lower lip was clamped between her teeth; there was something in her eyes that he had never seen before. Be careful, he told himself. Remember that if you go it's because of Pilar, not because of Megan.

"Please, Dad," Pilar said.

He nodded. "Florida it is," he said, and smiled when Pilar flung her arms around his neck.

Over her head he looked at Megan. She had let out the breath she'd been holding, and her eyes were bright with unshed tears.

It won't start again, he vowed. I won't let it.

And he wondered why his heart beat faster and his palms were suddenly damp.

"You're what?" Franco's face was mottled with rage.

"I'm going to Florida," Ricardo said. "With Megan and Pilar."

"You can't!" Franco began to pace up and down the narrow room. "*Dios mío,* do you realize what you're saying, Ricardo? You're going back to that woman again. I won't have it. She almost destroyed you. You—"

"I'm not going back to her. I'm going to Florida because of Pilar. She's my daughter, and I don't even know her."

"If you had married again, you might have had a son."

"But I didn't remarry. I have a daughter, and from now on she's going to be part of my life."

"She and her mother?"

"No! Neither Megan nor I have changed. It wouldn't work for us now any more than it worked for us before. But she's been kind enough to ask me to stay—"

"I bet she has!" Franco glared down at his son. "Mark my words, she'll do her best to seduce you into taking her back. That's why she came to Mexico. That's why she wants you to go to Florida."

As angry as his father now, Ricardo shook his head. But before he could say anything Franco said, "Sitting by your bedside, pretending she cared whether you lived or died."

Ricardo pushed himself up out of his chair. "I don't know why she came. I only know I'm damn glad she did and that she brought Pilar."

"She's using the girl to get you back. She's a conniving bitch. A—"

"That's enough!" The words were softly spoken, but Ricardo's eyes were like shards of hard, cold steel. "Megan is my wife. The mother of my child. No matter what our differences may have been, there was a time when we loved each other. I won't have you diminish that love. Nor will I allow you to speak about her as you just did."

"She tried to ruin your career."

"No. She didn't understand how important it was to me."

"She understood." Franco's lips curled in a snarl. "She knew how important it was to you, but that didn't matter. She wanted to be first in your life. She didn't care about your career or your family or anything else. She was a spoiled girl, a—"

"She was only twenty-one when we married. It was hard for her, living in a foreign country, trying to learn a new language, having a new husband, a baby. She'd never seen a bullfight in her life until after we were married. She didn't understand what my profession meant to me." Ricardo shook his head. "She was too young, too inexperienced. I asked too much of her."

"*You* asked too much!" Franco threw up his hands. "*Por Dios,* Ricardo, don't you see what's happening? The whole thing is starting again. She wants you back. Can't you see that? And she'll use whatever means she has to get what she wants—her child, the Florida sunshine, and yes, she'll use sex. She'll get you back into her bed the way she did before and you'll be fool enough to let her in." Hands balled into angry fists, Franco glared at his son. "Go to bed with her if you want to. Get it out of your system once and for all. But don't take her back. Whatever you do, don't take her back into your life again."

"I have no intention of letting Megan back into my life, Father. But whether I sleep with her or not won't be anybody's business but ours."

Franco opened his mouth, then snapped it shut. Without another word he went out and closed the door behind him.

Ricardo stared at the door, then, suddenly exhausted, he sank back down into the chair and buried his head in his hands. His father's words, *Don't take her back into your life again,* echoed in his mind. And his own words: *Whether I sleep with her or not . . .*

To sleep with Meggie. To make love with Meggie again.

He groaned aloud and tried to still the sudden tightening of his loins that the thought of being with her had stirred.

He would go to Florida because Pilar had asked him to. But he would be careful. Although he disagreed with his father on most things, he knew Franco was right about one thing. He mustn't let Meggie back into his life.

Pilar's powder-blue dress had a white lace collar and cuffs. Her new black shoes had one-inch heels.

"You look beautiful," Megan said when she finished braiding a blue ribbon through Pilar's braid. "Just beautiful."

"I hope my grandmother thinks so. I mean, I hope she'll like me."

"Of course, she'll like you."

"It's too bad Grandfather couldn't come."

"Yes, it is." Megan smoothed her hands down over the dove-gray silk dress she'd bought today after they left the hospital. She was relieved but not surprised that Franco hadn't wanted to come. But it was his loss. Pilar was his only grandchild, and she was a perfectly delightful little girl. He didn't know how much he was missing.

Just as Megan picked up the single strand of pearls she would wear with her dress, Isabel called out, "Fernando and Mother just drove up. Are you almost ready?"

"Yes," Megan called back. "We'll be right out." And to Pilar she said, "Ready?"

"I'm a little bit nervous."

"I know you are, honey, but it's going to be just fine. Your grandmother's going to love you. Okay?"

"Okay, Mom."

Megan kissed the tip of Pilar's nose, then, hand in hand, they went out to meet Ricardo's mother.

They were all in the living room. Fernando was at the bar, and Isabel was at the sideboard putting the finishing touches on the hors d'oeuvres. Josefa, as regal as a queen, sat poised on the edge of a velvet settee. Her hair, still as black as a crow's wings except for a two-inch streak of pure white that ran down the middle, had been pulled back and fastened with a high comb. She wore a black silk dress with a starchy white collar that was fastened in the front with a cameo.

"Buenas noches, Doña Josefa." Megan crossed the room and bent to kiss Josefa's cheek. "This is my daughter, Pilar. Pilar, this is your Grandmother Josefa."

"Buen... buenas noches, Abuela," Pilar said.

"You speak Spanish!" Josefa looked pleased.

"Yes, ma'am. I'm learning it in school."

"Muy bien. I speak only *un poquito,* a little English. We'll talk in both languages, yes?" She patted the place next to her. "Come and sit beside me, child. It's time we got acquainted."

Josefa took her hand. "Your father has told me he's going back to Florida with you and your mother. I think that's a fine idea. And I also think it's a fine idea that you're going to spend next summer with us. Do you know how to cook?"

"Yes, ma'am. Well, I can cook a little. I can make sandwiches and scrambled eggs, and sometimes I help Mom bake cakes." She shook her head. "But I can't make pies. Every time I try I get the dough all over the kitchen and on me."

Josefa laughed. "I can't make pies, either," she said. "But I can make very good bread. I'll teach you when you come next summer."

Pilar beamed a smile up at Josefa. She forgot her earlier shyness and warmed to her grandmother. They got along well with their mixture of Spanish and English, taught each other new words and laughed over their mistakes.

When Megan had a few moments alone with Josefa, Josefa took her hand and said, "You've done a wonderful job with Pilar, my dear. She's a lovely girl."

"Thank you, Doña Josefa."

"I'm sorry I've missed all of these years with that sweet child. I'm glad Ricardo is going back to Florida with you, Megan. It will be good for him to get to know Pilar and for her to know her father. She looks like him, don't you think?"

"Yes, I do."

"And you're going to let her come to visit us at the ranch next summer?"

Megan nodded. "If you think it'll be all right with Franco."

"It will be all right." Josefa hesitated. "My husband is a hard man, Megan, but a good man in his way. We've been married for almost fifty years, and I've never heard him raise his voice to me or to the children when they were small. But I know he can be difficult, and I certainly didn't approve of his attitude toward you. It was unjustified and unfair."

"It was because I'm not Mexican. Because I didn't understand about the bulls."

Josefa shook her head. "It wasn't entirely that. I don't think Franco would have approved of any woman Ricardo married. He wanted . . . he wants Ricardo to be faithful only to his profession. He doesn't want him to think of anything else, to do anything else. He wants him to give himself heart and soul to the bulls, to be the best *matador de toros* Mexico has ever produced." She gazed down at her hands. "He wants it for Ricardo because he couldn't attain it for himself."

"And when it's over?" Megan asked. "When Ricardo is forty, or forty-five, or fifty, what then?"

"He'll have the ranch. He'll raise brave bulls for other men, younger men, to fight." She looked at Megan. "He'll be lonely."

Megan covered the blue-veined, wrinkled hands with her own. She thought of the years ahead, for Ricardo and for herself.

Could there be a chance for them? A second chance at love? Or was it too late?

A sigh trembled through her. Perhaps . . . perhaps it wasn't too late.

Chapter 6

Dr. Cartas dismissed Ricardo five days before Christmas with the warning that he couldn't travel for at least a week.

"I'll stay at the ranch and spend Christmas with the family," Ricardo told Megan the day he left the hospital. "I'd like you and Pilar to come out and spend *Nochebuena,* Christmas Eve, with us. All of the family will be together that night, and I know Mother would love having you and Pilar there. We can leave for Florida on the twenty-sixth or seventh."

"Ricardo, ..." She didn't want to come right out and say, "I can't because of your father. Because I know he doesn't want me there." Trying to phrase her words carefully, she said, "I don't think it would be a good idea, Ricardo. Thank you for asking us, but—"

"I haven't spent a Christmas with Pilar since she was a baby," he said with a frown that drew his dark eyebrows together. "My mother and father are her grandparents. They have a right to get to know her, to spend time with her." He faced Megan, his face angry and set. "I want her with me this Christmas, Megan."

"All right!" Megan held her hands up in surrender. "Pilar can go with Isabel and Fernando. But if your father isn't nice to her, I'll—"

"Of course, he'll be nice to her. She's his granddaughter." He gripped Megan's shoulders. "He's not an ogre, Megan. I know the two of you never got along, but father's mellowed. He'll enjoy having Pilar with us, and so will Mother. And I want you to be with us, too, Megan. I want to spend Christmas with both of you."

He had the sudden urge to draw her into his arms. He wanted to rest his face against the softness of her hair, to have her put her arms around him and hold him the way she used to. He wanted to feel the warmth that he remembered.

Megan looked up at him, and there was an expression in her eyes that he couldn't quite read. Sadness? Regret? He didn't know, didn't want to know, so he let her go. "Plan to spend the night," he said. "We have dinner late, before midnight mass, and after church we all go back to the ranch for hot chocolate and *pan dulce*. It'll be too late to drive back to town."

She wanted to say, "No, I can't. I won't. I'm afraid to be that close to you again, especially with the warmth and the love that is Christmas." But she knew it wouldn't do any good to argue; Ricardo had decided. Both she and Pilar would spend Christmas Eve at the ranch.

* * *

Megan bought a new dress for Pilar and one for herself. Pilar's, in a lovely forest-green shade, with a delicate trim of lace around the collar, was ankle-length. When she tried it on, Megan smiled and said, "I'd love to have your picture taken in that dress, Pilar. You look like a painting of an old-fashioned girl. It's perfect."

"Do you think Dad will like it?"

"He'll love it."

"Can I wear my hair down instead of in a braid?"

"Of course, honey."

"And a little lipstick?"

"Of course . . . not!"

"Aw, Mom."

"Don't 'Aw, Mom' me." Megan grinned and held up the two dresses she was trying to choose from—one a plain black silk, the other a deep burgundy velvet. "Which one do you think?" she asked.

"The velvet," Pilar said.

Megan wasn't sure. The dress was a perfect fit, perhaps too perfect. It fell to midcalf, nipped in tight around her waist, and the neckline was more daring than she usually wore.

"Dad will love it," Pilar said.

"With your fair skin and blond hair it is truly beautiful on you, *Señora*." The saleswoman smiled. "You will take it, yes?"

Megan smiled back. "I'll take it, yes."

On Christmas Eve night when she and Pilar went into the living room where Isabel and Fernando were waiting, Isabel said, "Pilar looks as though she just stepped out of the pages of a fairy tale, Megan, and you look absolutely beautiful. I'm so glad you're going to spend Christmas with us. You can't imagine how excited Mama is to have you and Pilar with us. And don't worry about Father. It's going to be all right."

It was...all right. Nothing more, nothing less. Franco and Josefa were waiting for them in the patio where they could see the candles that had been placed in sanded paper bags all along the path that led to the house.

"Oh..." Pilar stopped. Her eyes were wide, shining, the way a child's eyes should be on Christmas Eve. She stood there in the center of the patio, gazing all around her at the purple bougainvillea that covered one whole section of the wall, at the water that bubbled up from the old stone fountain, at the scarlet poinsettia and at the lanterns that glowed from wall sconces.

"This is beautiful!" she said in an awed little voice. "I've never seen anything so beautiful."

Josefa came forward and hugged her. "It's your home, *mi hija*. Come now and say hello to your grandfather."

He had been standing in the shadows close to the house. Pilar looked up at the tall, grim-faced man who was her father's father. Her smile faded and her expression became as serious as his. *"Feliz Navidad, Abuelo,"* she said in a politely grave voice.

"Feliz Navidad." He looked over her head toward Megan. *"Feliz Navidad,"* he repeated to Megan, and before she could answer he took Pilar's hand and led her into the house where Ricardo waited.

He bent down and hugged Pilar. "Just look at you. That's a beautiful dress and you look beautiful in it."

"Mom wouldn't let me wear any lipstick."

"Good for her." He smoothed a hand over her fair hair. "Merry Christmas, *muchachita.*"

"Merry Christmas, Daddy," she answered, and his heart flooded with a joy unlike anything he'd ever known because this beautiful child was his daughter.

Megan came in, and it was all he could do not to go to her and take her in his arms. She had been lovely at twenty-one, but he hadn't realized until tonight what a stunningly beautiful woman she had become. She looked regally elegant in the velvet dress that did wonderful things for her figure. She'd worn her hair up, but wisps of it were loose around her face and golden tendrils drifted down her slender white neck. He wanted to encircle her neck with his hand and pull her gently toward him. He wanted . . . so many things.

He offered her his hand. "Come in."

The big living room was decorated with bright red ribbons, Christmas holly and Christmas candles. A fire glowed in the big stone fireplace, and a seven-foot Christmas tree stood in front of the windows that looked out over the mountains. Handel's *Messiah* played softly on a stereo.

"Come," Josefa said after warm mulled wine was served to the adults, "let's open the presents." She reached under the tree. "This one is for your mother, Pilar. Will you give it to her, please? And this is for your Aunt Isabel and your Uncle Fernando."

Megan smiled as she watched Pilar hand out the presents. She had bought a cashmere sweater for Isabel, gold filigree earrings for Josefa and white silk scarves for the three men, and Pilar was having a wonderful time passing them out.

"I've got an extra present for you, Dad," Pilar said when she handed Ricardo a package. "I had it specially printed."

"Printed?" He opened the Christmas-wrapped box, and when he folded back the white tissue paper, he lifted out a bright blue T-shirt, shook it out and smiled when he saw the words Welcome to Florida printed across the front. "Thank you, Pilar," he said with a laugh. "It's a wonderful present. I'll wear it my first day there."

"Now come here, child," Josefa said. "I have a gift for you." She handed Pilar a small beribboned box, and when Pilar opened it, she saw the cameo Josefa had been wearing the night she had come to dinner at Isabel's.

She looked up at her grandmother. "It's beautiful, *Abuela*," she said in a grave little voice. "I'll keep it forever."

"It belonged to my mother, and I wanted you to have it." Josefa smiled. "Come, let me pin it on your dress." And when she did, she drew Pilar to her and kissed her. *"Feliz Navidad, mi hija."*

Then Ricardo gave Pilar his present, a picnic basket filled with china plates, silverware and all kinds of delectable goodies. "For our fishing trips," he told her when she opened it.

Pilar's eyes grew round and large. She picked up jars of orange marmalade, strawberry preserves, peanut butter, pickles and olives. Cans of tuna, sardines, caviar, tins of crackers and cookies. "Oh, Dad," she said, and hugged him. "It's perfect! I could eat it all right now."

Ricardo laughed. "We'd better save it for that fishing trip. Right now we're going to have our Christmas dinner." When they started into the dining room, he put his hand on Megan's arm to hold her back from the others. He took a small box out of his pocket and handed it to her. "Merry Christmas," he said.

Surprised, she looked up at him, then untied the ribbon and lifted the lid. Inside, nestled on a bed of cotton, was a charm bracelet with five gold charms. She picked it up out of the box. There was a tiny, perfect flamenco dancer from Granada, the Tower of Gold from Sevilla, a filigree fan from Madrid, a golden orange from Valencia and a castle just like the one they had stayed in in Jaen.

She looked up at Ricardo, and tears like drops of crystal rose but didn't fall.

"For memories," Ricardo said. She tried to speak, but when she couldn't, he said again, "Merry Christmas, Megan." He hesitated, then, because he couldn't help himself, because it had been something he had wanted to do from the moment she had walked in the door tonight, he drew her into his arms and kissed her.

Her lips were soft and warm as she responded to him, and her arms came up to hold him as he held her. But only for a moment. When she stepped out of his embrace, she said, "Merry Christmas, Ricardo. And thank you. It's a lovely gift."

"Those were good days, Megan."

Her throat ached with the need to cry. "Yes," she whispered. "I'll never forget. I loved..." She swallowed hard, wanting to say, "I loved you then." Instead she said, "I loved Spain."

He touched her cheek. "And I loved you."

She felt as though she were drowning in the depths of his amber eyes. She swayed toward him. Hands against his chest, she said, "We'd...we'd better go in."

"Yes." But still he didn't move. Her face was close to his. He wanted to kiss her again. But he didn't.

The table was laden with food. There was roast turkey with dressing, and baked ham, as well as typical holiday Mexican dishes.

"This is *bacalao,* codfish." Franco passed it to Pilar.

She looked at it, polite enough not to wrinkle her nose, and said, "I think I already have enough of everything."

"Have a taste at least," he said testily.

Pilar put a small piece on her plate. Franco watched with a frown. She took a small bite. He waited. She took another bite and smiled. "It's delish!" she announced.

"Let me give you a little more."

"Okay." She grinned up at him. "It sure tastes better than it looks."

Josefa, watching the exchange from the other end of the table, smiled.

The Spanish colonial church in San Rafael had been built in the year 1650. Time had weathered the old stone and given it a look that was both picturesque and stately. By the time the Montoya family arrived at the church, it was almost filled. There were families dressed much like the Montoyas, men in dark suits, women in their best dresses. And others, poor ranchers, street vendors, maids and gardeners and beggars, most of them with their children and babies.

Roses, poinsettia, white calla lilies and tall white candles surrounded the altar. At one side there was a crèche: Mary, her head covered in a blue rebozo, like the Indian women who had come to worship this

Christmas Eve; Joseph, and the baby Jesus who lay cradled on a bed of straw; and shepherds with their sheep watching at one side of the palm-thatched stable.

"It's beautiful, isn't it?" Pilar whispered to her father.

"Yes, it is." He squeezed her hand and waited until Megan went into the pew next to Isabel and Fernando, then motioned for Pilar to sit next to her mother and came in beside her.

From the balcony above, the organ began to play. The lights in the church were dimmed, and there was only the illumination from candles as the adult choir, then a choir of children, came down the center aisle, followed by the priest and three young acolytes.

The congregation stood and the service began.

It was all so achingly familiar, Megan thought. The candles, the scent of incense and lilies, the music. She closed her eyes and let it flow over her, glad now that she had come and that she and Pilar were sharing this special time with Ricardo and his family.

But there was sadness, too, because of all the years she had deprived Pilar of the warmth and closeness of her Mexican family. Her own parents had died four years before; Josefa and Franco were the only grandparents Pilar had.

All these years she had told herself she had been right to keep Pilar away from Ricardo and his family, but she knew now that she had been wrong, and for that she was bitterly sorry.

When it was time to kneel, Megan knelt and closed her eyes. Resting her head on her clasped hands, she prayed a silent prayer for forgiveness and for healing of the years father and daughter had been apart.

The choir began to sing "Adeste Fideles." She felt Pilar's hand tentatively touch hers, and clasped it. And when she lifted her head, she saw that Pilar was holding Ricardo's hand, too, and that they were, for this brief time, united as a family.

By the time they had eaten the variety of sweet breads Josefa had prepared that day, along with steaming cups of *atole* and hot chocolate, it was after three and Pilar had fallen asleep in her chair.

"It's late," Josefa said. "Time for the child to be in bed."

"Time for all of us to be in bed." Isabel yawned and reached for Fernando's hand. "Merry Christmas. We'll see you in the morning, or afternoon."

"Yes, it's late." Ricardo pushed back from the table and bent over Pilar. But when he started to pick her up, Franco said, "No, she's too heavy. You must be careful of your back." He picked her up, and she stirred and murmured a protest. *"Ya, ya, niña, está bien,"* he said, and she slid her arm around his neck and snuggled against his chest.

His mouth twitched, but his expression was unreadable as he carried her down the long, arched corridor that led to the bedrooms.

"Pilar and Megan are in the room next to mine," Ricardo said, and when they reached the right room, he stood aside so that his father could go in.

Franco placed Pilar on one of the twin beds. Just for a moment he stood looking down at her, the same unreadable expression on his face, then without a word to either Ricardo or Megan he turned and left the room.

"I think our daughter is winning his heart," Ricardo said softly.

Our daughter. Because she wanted to hide all that she was feeling, Megan bent down to take Pilar's shoes off.

"Wait." Ricardo touched her arm.

Megan looked at him. "It's very late."

"But it's not *too* late." His eyes were intense, questioning. "Is it, Megan?"

"I . . . I don't know, Ricardo. I—"

"You know." He cupped the back of her slender neck and drew her close. Before she could move away he kissed her.

And as they had before, Megan's lips softened and parted under his. He drew her closer. She felt the tip of his tongue against her lips, and answered his touch with hers.

The kiss deepened and her body warmed. She put her arms around his shoulders and felt the tension in his hard, lean body. "Ricardo," she whispered against his lips. "Ricardo."

He held her away and looked down at her. His eyes were like fire, his expression unreadable. He tightened his hands on her shoulders.

"Merry Christmas, Megan," he murmured. And before she could answer he let her go and hurried out of the room.

Two days later they left for Florida.

Chapter 7

Megan offered Ricardo his choice of one of the efficiencies or the boat, and he chose the boat. The *Sea Chum* was a thirty-two-foot motor-sailer, and while the living space wasn't as big as the efficiency, he liked it. The galley was equipped with a two-burner stove, a microwave, a small refrigerator and a compact dining area. In the small salon there were built-in bookcases, two easy chairs and a padded bench along the side that could be used as an extra bunk.

The bed in the cabin was comfortable, and he liked going to sleep with the gentle slap of waves against the bow and the good salt-smell of the sea.

Every morning he ran for two miles. There were times when the weakness in his legs returned and he had to push himself. That made him impatient, and the next day he pushed even harder.

He liked Florida and he loved being able to spend time with Pilar. She was a seven-year-old charmer, an enchanting child, half Megan, half him, eager and bright and joyful.

Every morning before she left for school she ran down the dock to his boat. She'd give him a funny little salute and call out, "Permission to come aboard, sir."

Grinning, he'd return the salute and answer, "Permission granted." She'd have a couple sips of his coffee, give him a quick hug and off she'd go, dressed in blue jeans and a shirt, her long blond braid flapping down against her back.

At first he didn't approve of her wearing jeans to school because he was used to seeing children in Mexico and Spain dressed in uniforms, usually navy blue with starched white shirts, knee-length socks and polished shoes. But Pilar's clothes suited her; she simply wasn't a starched-white-shirt kind of little girl.

After she left for school, he helped Megan's hired man with whatever chores needed to be done. Tyrone Wadsworth, who had been born and raised in the Keys, had worked for Megan for the five years she'd owned La Gaviota. In addition to his work around the motel he took care of the boats that came in and out and acted as skipper of Megan's charter fishing boat.

During Ricardo's first week there, Tyrone had little to say to him, but that changed one early morning when Ricardo came in from his run to find Tyrone on the docks, hands on his hips, using words in English that Ricardo had never heard before. When Ricardo asked what the matter was, Tyrone pushed his sweat-stained, wide-brimmed straw hat back on his head and said, "Damn snowbird bunch of highfalutin, good for nothin', no-count businessmen." He pointed at the dirty, blood-spattered deck. "I took 'em out fishin' a couple of days ago and they acted all right. Drank a hell of a lot of rum, but I'm partial to rum myself so that didn't bother me none. Yesterday mornin' they wanted to take the boat out again, but I said it was my day off." Tyrone swiped at the sweat that ran down his bare chest. "I got me a little mama down in Tavernier I visit once a week, and I sure hidey didn't want to miss seein' her. I found out when we were fishin' that a couple of them knew almost as much about runnin' the boat as I did, so I finally agreed to let 'em take her out alone."

He spit off the dock. "Don't know what all they did. Had a bunch of women on. Everybody drinkin' and fightin' and Lord only knows what. Down below it looks like they was sloppin' hogs. I gotta fix it all up 'fore Miss Megan sees it, or she'll give me sure-hidey for lettin' them take it out alone."

"I'll be glad to help," Ricardo said.

Tyrone looked him up and down. "It's a dirty job. You up to it?"

"I'm up to it."

Tyrone was right: it was one hell of a dirty job and it took them most of the day. When it was done, they sat up on the bow of the boat and drank a couple of beers.

"I heard you was married to Miss Megan a long time ago," Tyrone said. "Ain't none of my business, but she's a mighty fine woman. Can't figure why a man would leave her or that precious young'un."

"She left me," Ricardo said.

"Then I reckon you musta done somethin' mighty bad."

"I did," Ricardo took a swallow of his beer. "I fought bulls."

"Bulls!" Tyrone looked startled. "You one of them fellas wears the funny pants and waves a red cape around?"

Ricardo's mouth tightened. "I am a matador, yes."

"I'll be danged." Tyrone drained his beer and reached for another can. He popped it, drank, then shook his head. "I reckon that's a right dangerous thing to do."

"Sometimes."

"You been hurt bad? Is that why you're here now? Come to get recuperated?"

Ricardo nodded.

"Must take some kinda balls to do what you do." He looked at Ricardo with new respect. "You want another beer?"

After that he and Tyrone were friends. Ricardo helped with the dock work, rigged lines and pumped gas for the boats that tied up at the dock. He liked being out in the sun and working beside Tyrone, but the highlight of his day was when the school bus returned Pilar home in the afternoon. He loved hearing how her day had been, how a boy named Willie Bob Benson had pulled her braid and called her skinny, and that she'd gotten an A plus for the composition she'd written about her visit to Mexico.

But if Pilar was communicative, Megan wasn't. She was pleasant but reserved, as he was with her. When the motel was busy, she worked in the office with her manager, a skinny, dour-faced woman named Agnes Zeller who, when Megan introduced them, had looked him up and down suspiciously.

"You from Mexico?" she asked.

And when Ricardo said he was, she pursed her lips and wrinkled her nose.

He saw little of Megan during the day. When he did see her, she would wave, then disappear into one of the rooms or into her own apartment. It was as though they were both walking on eggs, Ricardo thought. As though they weren't quite sure how to handle this new situation they found themselves in.

He told himself this was the way they both wanted it, that theirs was a precarious relationship at best, and that they both knew he was here only because of Pilar. He didn't want to make a mistake. He wanted to go slowly.

But there were times when he awoke in the night with the thought of how Megan had felt in his arms on that early Christmas morning, and of the way her lips had parted under his. He'd think of the softness of her mouth and how her arms had come around to hold him close. And his body would tighten with need.

It was a particular kind of pain to sit across the table from her night after night, or to see her working in the yard, wearing tight little shorts that cupped her bottom, a sheen of sweat on the long, bare legs, legs that were as beautiful as he remembered.

He remembered so many things...what it had been like to make love with her in the golden sunlight of a Spanish morning. The way her eyes grew smoky when he touched her, the sweet, small gasp when their bodies joined, the frantic, reaching movements when she lifted her body to his. He remembered every whispered moan, every sigh. Every final cry.

Sometimes at night when he couldn't sleep he would sit out on the bow of the boat, alone except for one old pelican that came to rest on one of the dock stanchions each night. He would think of how it would be if Meggie were here with him, looking at the stars with him, listening to the slap of waves against the hull. He would imagine what he would do if some night she came down the dock to the boat, what it would be like if they went below to the cabin.

When thoughts of Meggie, of her being so near and yet so far, made his body grow hard with want and need, he would strip off his clothes and dive naked into the water. He would swim until his muscles ached and his breath came hard and gasping. Until the wanting ebbed.

But every day his hunger sharpened and grew.

Three weeks after their return from Mexico, on a bright and sunny Saturday morning, they took the *Sea Chum* out for a weekend sail.

"We'll go down toward Long Key," Pilar told Ricardo when Tyrone cast off the line. "You and I can fish while Mom runs the boat. Okay?"

"*Más que* okay, more than okay." Ricardo put his arm around her in a quick squeeze and smiled over at Megan. She looked as beautiful and as fresh as the morning in trim white shorts and a red T-shirt, and she seemed more relaxed with him this morning than she had been before.

She handled the boat like an expert, and stood at the wheel, long, slender legs sturdy and strong, feet braced against the roll of the boat.

He tried not to look at her legs, but concentrated instead on rigging the fishing lines. He and Pilar trolled for almost two hours. Pilar caught a mackerel and a jack; he didn't even have a bite.

"That's okay," Pilar said. "These two are enough for lunch. But you can clean 'em, okay?"

"*Sí*, okay. That's only fair since you caught them."

They anchored in one of the coves a little while later, and after he cleaned the fish, Pilar said, "It's hot, Mom. Can Dad and I go swimming now?"

"Sure." Megan smiled at her daughter. "You two go on. I'll start lunch."

"No, you don't," Ricardo said. "The three of us will swim, then I'll help you fix lunch. You brought a suit, didn't you?"

"Yes, but—"

"Come on, Mom. It'll be more fun with the three of us." Pilar looked at Ricardo. "Have you got a suit?"

"I've got it on under my jeans, *muchacha*. You and your mother go down below and change. I'll meet you in the water."

When they disappeared down the steps, he took his jeans off and, balancing himself on the side of the boat, raised his arms above his head and dived in. After the heat of the sun, the water felt so cool against his skin that he gasped. He swam hard toward shore, then back to the boat and saw Megan and Pilar standing on the bow. He laughed when Pilar held her nose and jumped into the water feet first, but the laughter died when he saw Megan poised on the bow. Her white bikini was a startling contrast to her tan. Her body was lithe and firm, her high breasts fuller than he remembered. She was incredibly beautiful, infinitely desirable.

He watched her arch her arms over her head, then she dived, cut into the water clean and true and shot to the surface. She brushed the water out of her eyes and looked around for Pilar, and for him.

"It's wonderful!" she said. "And the day! Isn't it an absolutely perfect day?"

He tried not to get too close to her, but that was difficult. There were just the three of them, here in this deserted cove. Pilar teased and, pretending to be a fish, she dived down and nipped her mother's ankle. Megan screamed and, without thinking, threw her arms around his neck. He put his arms around her, holding her. The scream died and they looked into each other's eyes.

"Meggie," he said just as Pilar bobbed to the surface.

She broke away from him. "I . . . I'd better go back and start lunch." Then she turned and swam toward the boat.

By the time he and Pilar came in, the table had been set out in the bow and lunch was almost ready. He boosted Pilar aboard, then hefted himself up onto the boat.

"That was great, wasn't it?" Pilar reached for a towel. "Now I'm so hungry I could eat a—" She stopped. "Dad?" She pointed to the part of the scar, still jagged and raw-looking, that came above the line of his black bikini trunks. "Is that . . . is that where you were hurt? Is that where the bull . . . ?" Her face went pale, and she sank down into a deck chair.

Megan, who'd just come up from the galley with a tray of food, stopped midway on the step.

"That's . . . that's awful. It . . ." Pilar's eyes were wide with shock. She started to shake.

In two strides Ricardo crossed the deck and knelt beside her. "It's better now, *muchachita*," he said. "The wound was healed. Really, I'm all better now."

"But your . . ." Pilar took a shaking breath. "Your stomach is all cut there." Her voice rose, high, out of control. "The scar's all red and funny where the . . . the bull...where his horns..." She gulped and covered her eyes with her hands.

"*Niña*, don't." Ricardo put his arms around her. "Oh, baby, don't. I'm fine now, Pilar. Truly." He pressed the back of her head against his shoulder, rocking her, soothing her.

She looked up at him. "How come...how come you do it, Daddy? I don't understand."

He looked up and saw Meggie standing on the steps leading up from the galley. He saw the shock in her eyes, and suddenly it was Meggie saying the same words that Pilar had said: "Why do you do it? I don't understand."

He whispered her name. She didn't answer, but turned and went back down to the galley.

She put the tray down. From above she heard Ricardo say, "Bullfighting is what I do, Pilar. I've been doing it for a very long time, and this was the first time I was ever hurt this badly."

"I think...I think it's terrible," she heard her daughter say.

And Ricardo answered, "You've seen football games, haven't you? Have you ever seen a player get hurt?"

"Yes, but—"

"Or a prizefight on television. Or car races? A lot of those men get hurt, too, Pilar."

"Not like you," she said. "Not like you, Daddy."

Megan gripped the edge of the sink. She took a deep breath and called out, "Lunch is ready. How about some help down here?"

Ricardo came to the top step. "Hand me my shirt." She did, and when he buttoned it to cover the scar, he said, "I'm sorry about what just happened."

Megan nodded. "I know. Pilar will be all right. I was."

"Megan . . . I'm sorry. I . . ." He lifted his shoulders in a helpless gesture and shook his head.

She started to pick up a bowl of potato salad, but then she hesitated. "Don't look like that," she murmured. "It's going to be all right."

"I shouldn't have let her see the scar," he said in a low voice. "I forgot."

"That means you're feeling better." She laid one hand against the side of his face. "Go on now or the fish will get cold."

He took hold of her wrist and held her hand there for a moment longer, then he pressed his lips, and his tongue, against her palm.

"No," Megan said in a low, strangled voice. And he let her go.

Pilar had little to say during lunch. She just kept looking at Ricardo.

Finally he said, "I need some catsup on my fish."

Pilar jumped up before he could move and said, "I'll get it."

He raised an eyebrow at Megan when Pilar disappeared down into the galley. "Now she thinks I'm an invalid," he muttered.

"You aren't an invalid, but you are recuperating. Let her help you if she wants to, Ricardo. I think it's something she needs to do. To feel a part of you. To—"

"She is a part of me, a part of both of us, Megan. The best part."

Pilar bounded up the galley steps. "Here, Dad." She plunked the catsup down in front of him. "Is there anything else you want? Another glass of iced tea maybe?''

"No, Pilar. But if there is, I'll tell you."

"Okay." She took a bite of her fish. "Maybe after we eat you ought to rest for a while."

He pretended to consider that. "Maybe I will."

It was a lazy, hazy afternoon with just enough wind to billow the sails. Megan stood at the wheel. Pilar, cross-legged on a mat, did her homework, and Ricardo stretched out and went to sleep. A little before dark they pulled in to Lower Matecumbe Key and anchored.

The wind had died. The sea was calm and golden in the last rays of the sun. As they watched, the sky turned from blue to brilliant pink that stretched in streaks of color as far as they could see.

"We'll anchor here and spend the night," Megan said. "I've got cold cuts and enough potato salad left for dinner."

"But we could have that for lunch tomorrow." Pilar turned her attention to her father. "There's a really great restaurant in Matecumbe, Dad. They make terrific cheeseburgers and fries."

He raised his eyebrows and looked at Megan.

"They also have wonderful shrimp cocktails and inch-and-a-half-thick steaks," she said with a smile.

"Do I need a tie?"

"Nobody in the Keys ever needs a tie." Megan waited. "So what'll it be? Cheeseburgers and steaks or baloney sandwiches?"

They dressed—Megan and Pilar in clean shorts and shirts, Ricardo in jeans and the bright blue T-shirt Pilar had given him for Christmas—and took the dinghy to shore. The restaurant wasn't fancy. There were wooden floors, checkered clothes on the tables and paper napkins. But Pilar said her cheeseburger was the best she'd ever had, and the steaks were as thick as Megan had promised.

Ricardo and Megan had a bottle of red wine with their dinner, Pilar had root beer, and they all had key lime pie for dessert. By the time they finished and Ricardo rowed them back to the boat, Pilar was yawning. She gave him a hug, said, "Night, Dad" and went below with Megan to the cabin.

Five minutes later Megan came back on deck carrying two mugs of coffee. "She was asleep as soon as her head hit the pillow," she told Ricardo. "She'll go like a dynamo all day, then suddenly she folds."

Ricardo took the coffee from her and they settled into the deck chairs. An offshore breeze cooled the air. A golden slice of new moon and a sky full of stars softened the night. Porpoise frolicked in the still waters between shore and boat while white ibis fed in the shallows.

"I'm sorry you have to sleep out on the deck tonight," Megan said. "You could sleep on the bunk in the salon if you'd rather."

Ricardo shook his head. "It's a beautiful night. Besides, I often spend the night out here."

"You do?" She sounded surprised.

Ricardo nodded. "On nights when I can't sleep."

"I didn't know you had difficulty sleeping."

"Sometimes." He put his coffee mug down. "When I think about you."

Megan's hands tightened around her mug.

"I think of you there in the apartment. I think of you in bed—"

"Don't," she said.

"And I remember the way it was when things were good between us. I remember Spain."

"Ricardo—"

"I think what it would be like to hold you again. To make love to you again."

"No!" With a strangled cry she got up and went to stand at the rail. With unseeing eyes she looked out over the still water. I won't let it start again, she told herself. I won't let myself in for that kind of pain again. I remember Spain, he'd said. Well, so did she. She remembered every sunlit morning, every moonlight kiss. She remembered his body over hers, the whispered words of passion, the ecstasy. She remembered everything.

"Meggie?" He came to stand beside her. "Don't shut me out. I need you. I—" With a strangled cry he pulled her into his arms.

Then his mouth was on hers and he kissed her with all of the hunger and all of the passion he'd held in check since Christmas Eve at the ranch.

Her body was stiff, her lips compressed. She wouldn't yield. She wouldn't...

He rained kisses over her face, her eyes, her nose, her cheeks. He took her mouth again, and when her lips wouldn't soften under his, he took her lower lip between his teeth to bite and suckle. He kissed the corners of her mouth, and when she whispered in protest, he thrust his tongue against hers. She moaned low in her throat, then, with a small cry, reached her arms around him hard and held him as he was holding her.

"Oh, Meggie," he said against her lips. *"Mi amor, mi vida."*

"Oh, please," she said, not sure what it was she was asking of him. But, oh, it was heaven to be held by him like this, to feel the press of his body so close to hers.

He put one hand against the small of her back to bring her closer, and she moaned against his lips.

"No," she whispered. "No, please. Let me go."

But when he took his hand away, she didn't move. She felt his hardness and began to move against it, hungry and hot for him, unable to stop because she wanted more. So much more.

He opened the buttons of her shirt and cupped her breasts. He thrust his leg between her legs and took her muffled cry of protest into his mouth. And he thought he would go crazy if he couldn't have her.

She couldn't get enough of his kisses, of his mouth. It was as though they had never been apart. Everything about him was familiar, dear. She pulled the T-shirt up and thrust her hands under it because she had to feel his skin. She tangled her fingers through the thatch of chest hair, then buried her face there. She licked his skin and tasted salt. She reached around to cup his buttocks, to pull him even tighter, closer.

"Dios, Meggie. Ah, Meggie, *por Dios!* I can't wait. Now, Meggie. Please now." He held her away from him. "Here. On the mat. Yes?"

She looked up at him, dazed by need, drunk with desire.

He kicked off his sneakers. He loosened his belt and tugged the jeans down over his hips.

She saw his scar.

"Oh, no," she whispered. "What am I doing? Oh, Lord."

He reached for her, but before he could stop her she ran to the railing, swung herself over and dived into the water.

Salt tears and saltwater stung her eyes. She wanted Ricardo with every cell, every pore, every part of her body. She wanted to make love with him. She would go crazy if she didn't.

They could. They were still legally man and wife. Pilar was asleep in the cabin. There was nothing to stop them. There would be nothing wrong, and yet... And yet she couldn't do it. For nothing had changed. He was still Ricardo, a matador of *toros*. When he recovered from this last goring, he would go back to Mexico. Back to his world, a world she couldn't bear to live in with him.

She looked back at the boat and saw him leaning against the rail there. "I love you," she said, because she knew he couldn't hear. "I will always love you."

She looked up at the stars, and a sadness unlike anything she had ever known shook her to the very depths of her being because she knew she couldn't change. Nor could he.

In a path of silver moonlight she swam back to the boat. Ricardo gave her his hand to help her aboard, then he let her go. She didn't look at him, and when she accepted the towel he gave her, she busied herself drying off.

"You'd better get out of those wet clothes," he said in a voice devoid of any emotion.

"Yes, I will. I..." She looked up at him, up into his amber eyes. "I'm sorry," she said, and before he could answer she turned and hurried below to the cabin.

Chapter 8

During the days that followed their weekend sailing trip, Megan did everything she could to avoid Ricardo. On the nights that Pilar invited him to their apartment for dinner she put the meal on the table and pleaded a headache, a suddenly remembered appointment in town, or motel business that had to be attended to. She pretended she didn't see the questioning look in her daughter's eyes, or the tightening of Ricardo's jaw whenever she made her excuses.

She slept badly at night, and when she couldn't sleep, she would stand by her window looking out toward the *Sea Chum,* wondering if he was asleep, or if he, too, found sleep impossible. He had said that on the nights when he couldn't sleep he sat up on the deck, thinking about her, wanting her. As she wanted him.

She tried not to think how painfully close she had come to giving in to him and to the terrible demands of her body that night on the boat. She wasn't sure even now whether she was glad she had stopped or sorry. She only knew it would have been a mistake for both of them because nothing had changed. Ricardo would still risk his life every time he stepped into a bullring and she would always be afraid. And she couldn't help that. She was glad for Pilar's sake that he had come to Florida, but for her sake, and for his, she wished he hadn't.

So she wasn't surprised when, a week after the sailing trip, he said he wanted to return to Mexico.

Because it was Agnes Zeller's day off, Megan was in the motel office alone when he came in.

"It's time I went back to Mexico," he said without preamble. "I've loved being here with Pilar, and with you, but it's time I went home."

He clenched his hands at his sides. For the past few weeks his home had been here with his daughter and wife. Never mind that he and Megan were separated—in his heart and mind she was his wife. If he lived to be a hundred, that was how it would be. That wouldn't change, not for him.

But it had changed for Megan, and because it had he knew he could no longer stay. He wanted her and he thought that she wanted him. But he didn't think she would ever give in to whatever emotion it was she felt. For her sake, as well as his, he would leave.

"It's time for me to go home," he said.

"But Pilar..." Megan wet her lips. "Pilar has gotten used to your being here. She loves being with you, Ricardo."

"And I love being with her." He picked up a folder that advertised the dolphin show in Islamorada and pretended to study it. "June's only four months away.

Pilar will visit me at the ranch then, if you haven't changed your mind about letting her come.''

"I haven't changed my mind.'' She looked at him across the reception desk. "I wish you wouldn't go. Pilar loves having you here.''

"I can't stay, Megan. I want you so much that it's torture being with you every day and not being able to touch you, to hold you.'' He shook his head. "I can't take it anymore. I'm sorry. I have to leave.''

She came around the desk. "I wish things were different. I wish...''

"Yes, so do I.'' He ran his hands up and down her arms, and because he couldn't help himself, he drew her closer. "Oh, Meggie,'' he said, and kissed her.

She said no. She thought she said no. But her lips parted under his, and when he touched her tongue, she shivered and moaned low in her throat.

"I want you,'' he said. "Lord, Meggie, don't you know how much I want you?'' He brought her closer. "Don't you know? Can't you tell how much I need you?'' He cupped her bottom and brought her hard against him. Her body was warm and soft against his. If he tugged the white shorts down, he could slip his hands under her panties, feel her, touch her. He knew by the way she answered his kiss, by the way her body trembled against his, how soft she would feel, how moist and ready.

He half lifted her, raising her up so that their bodies touched there, and pressed her harder, closer, moving her against him until she whimpered in her need and cried out, "Oh, please. Please.''

"Your apartment,'' he whispered against her lips.

"Yes.'' She took his mouth, frantic in her need. "Yes! Oh, yes, I...''

Tires crunched on the gravel driveway outside. A door slammed. With a smothered moan Megan stepped away from him. He turned his back when a man and a woman came in.

"How do, Miz Quinn," the man said. "You 'member us? Mr. and Miz Claybourne from Tuscaloosa?"

"Of course, Mr. Claybourne." She clenched her hands tightly to her side so that he wouldn't see she was trembling. "It's...it's nice to see both of you again."

"You got our letter, saying we were coming?"

"Yes, I did." She stepped around to the other side of the desk. She looked toward Ricardo, then away. "I've got a nice waterfront room all ready for you. It's the same one you had last year."

"Good, good. How's old Tyrone?"

"He's fine, Mr. Claybourne."

"You reckon he can take me and the missus out fishing tomorrow?"

"Yes, I'm sure he can."

He filled out the registration card, shook hands with Megan, nodded in Ricardo's direction and held the door open for his wife.

The office was quiet.

"Ricardo?" Megan gripped the edge of the desk. Her face was pale, her eyes sad.

"I know," he said. "You don't have to say anything."

"I'm sorry."

He nodded.

"When...when will you leave?"

"By the end of the week."

"Do you want me to tell Pilar?"

He shook his head. "No, I'll tell her."

"I'm sorry," she said again.

"So am I, Meggie." His gaze rested on her face for a moment before he turned and went back out into the sunlight.

Pilar ran out to the boat as soon as she got home from school that day. "Guess what Willie Bob did today?" she asked as soon as she hugged him. "He passed me a note during geography. Know what it said?"

"I can't even guess."

"It said . . ." She rolled her eyes and giggled. "It said, 'I love you.'"

"I love you?"

"Yes!" Giggling and slapping her knees, she rocked back and forth in the deck chair. "Willie Bob Benson! Ugh! Yech!"

Ricardo smiled. "Is he that bad?"

"He's horrible! He's got carrot-colored hair and freckles all over his face. And he belches! Last year I caught a bigger bonefish than he did and I will this year, too." She grinned up at Ricardo. "You and me together, Dad. We'll beat everybody. The fishing tournament is the weekend after next."

"Pilar, I . . ." He tried to think of the words to tell her that he was leaving. "Honey, I . . . I don't think I'll be here then."

The grin faded. "What . . . what do you mean?"

"I have to get back to Mexico, Pilar."

"But you said you were going to be here for four or five months."

"I know, honey, but—"

"You promised to go bonefishing with me!"

"We can go tomorrow."

"I have to go to school tomorrow." Her chin wobbled. "Why do you have to go? Is it because of Mom? Have you had a fight? Have you—?"

"No, of course not." Ricardo began to pace up and down the deck. "It's nothing like that, Pilar. It's just that I need to get back to Mexico."

"But why? You're not all better yet. The places where you were hurt, the scar...that's still not better." Her eyes filled with tears. "Are you going back to fight another bull?"

"No, sweetheart. Not for a long time."

"I thought you liked it here. I thought you loved us."

He came closer and squatted down beside her. "I do love you. I love you more than anything in the world."

She sniffed. "Mom, too?"

"Pilar—"

"If you do, then how come you're leaving?"

How could he explain to this precious child of his that as much as he loved her he couldn't stay, that it was torture being around her mother because her mother no longer loved him?

"You're going to come to Mexico next summer," he said. "I'll teach you to ride and—"

"But next summer's so far away," she wailed.

"Only a few months."

"I don't want you to go!" She threw her arms around his neck and began to cry. "Don't go, Dad," she wept. "Please don't go."

He felt as though his heart were breaking. "Don't cry, baby. Please don't cry."

"When..." She swiped at her nose with the back of her hand. "When will you go?"

"Thursday or Friday." He held her away from him. "Do you have a lot of homework today?"

"Not too much."

"Then why don't you go do it, and when you finish, you and I will go someplace special for dinner. Just the two of us, okay?"

She stood up, but she didn't look at him. "Guess I'd better go."

"I'll see you in a little while." He picked her up and put his arms around her. "I love you, Pilar."

"And I love you, Daddy." She squeezed him hard and the tears started again. "I wish you were here all the time. I wish you lived with us, with Mom and me."

"So do I, *muchachita*." He kissed her teary cheeks and put her down. "Don't cry anymore. Okay?"

She sniffed. "Okay," she said, and gave him one of her funny little salutes before she turned and jumped down to the dock and ran back toward the motel and the apartment she and her mother shared.

Ricardo turned away and looked out over the water. Tears stung his eyes. He ran a hand across his face. He loved this child of his, loved her so much that it tore at his insides. But because there wasn't any other way, he would leave her.

He made a reservation to fly out of Miami on Aeromexico on Friday morning. Megan would drive him to the airport after Pilar left for school.

It's for the best, he told himself, and tried not to notice how solemn and sad his daughter had looked since he had told her he was leaving.

He planned a fishing trip on Wednesday, and when she got out of school, Tyrone had the charter boat ready to go.

The three of them fished until it was dark. Ricardo caught four king mackerel, and Tyrone caught two red snappers that he fixed for their dinner, along with a conch salad, hush puppies and hot biscuits.

Pilar had little to say, but Tyrone talked about the old days in the Keys when there hadn't been more than a few fishing shacks between Jewfish Creek and Key West.

"The fishin' was better then," he said. "Snowbirds mostly came down in the winter to fish. Now everybody comes down every damn month of the year. Just too dang many fancy hotels and fancy folks. Ain't like it used to be."

It was almost nine when they took the boat back in. "Your momma's gonna skin my hide for keepin' you out so late," Tyrone told Pilar. "You take her the fish we caught and maybe it'll be okay." He looked up toward the motel. "I see her out on your porch, so you best run along."

She took the string of fish that he'd cleaned. "Thanks, Tyrone." She looked up at Ricardo. "Night, Dad."

"Good night, sweetheart." He kissed her cheek. "I had a great time tonight."

"Me, too. We could do it all the time if you stayed."

"Pilar—"

"I gotta go," she said. "See ya."

"That's a mighty fine little girl." Tyrone leaned against the railing. "She sure hidey is going to miss you."

"I'll miss her, too."

"I reckon you will." Tyrone sighed. "You go on to bed, Mr. Ricardo. I'll clean up the boat."

But Ricardo shook his head. He helped Tyrone swab the deck and hose down the dock, and finally, close to midnight, he told Tyrone good-night and went back to the *Sea Chum*.

But it was a long time before he went to sleep. And when he did, it was to dream of Megan, and of Pilar, who kept saying over and over again, "How come you gotta go, Daddy? How come?"

He packed on Thursday morning. At noon Megan came down to the boat to invite him for dinner that night.

"It's your last night," she said. "We . . . Pilar and I, we want you to come. She got up early this morning and baked you a chocolate cake." A slight smile curved the corners of her mouth. "It's a little lopsided and the frosting ran. Don't say anything."

"I won't." Ricardo swallowed hard and, trying to keep his expression even, asked, "What time shall I come?"

"Six-thirty. That will give her time to get her homework done before dinner."

He didn't want to go. He didn't want to sit across from his wife and daughter and pretend everything was all right, that they were a family. He didn't want to pretend not to see the strain on Megan's face or the disappointment in Pilar's eyes. Tomorrow he would leave, and that would be the end of whatever hope he had that someday he and Megan might work out their differences.

"Will you be there? During dinner I mean?" he asked. "You won't suddenly get a headache or have to go to a meeting in town?"

Hot color crept into her cheeks. "Of course, I'll be there. Come at six. We'll have a drink."

Ricardo nodded. "At six."

After she left, he finished packing. And when that was done, he went for one final walk on the beach. He liked Florida, especially here in the Keys, for although as Tyrone had said, the Keys had changed, there was still much that would be forever constant. Nowhere else in the world were the waters this particular shade of blue; nowhere were clouds whiter and fuller. There was nothing more pleasing to the eye than the sight of great blue herons, snowy egrets and roseate spoonbills feeding in the shallows at twilight. Or the brilliantly beautiful sunsets, red and gold against the deep blue of the sky. He would miss the way the moon rose over the water, the sea grape and palms, pond cypress and royal poinciana. Hush puppies and key lime pie.

But most of all he would miss Megan and his daughter.

When it began to spatter rain and he saw that it was almost three, he turned and started back toward the motel. Pilar would be home soon. If she came down to the boat, they would have a soft drink and he would send her home to do her homework and then begin to get ready for tonight. His last night.

It was raining harder by the time he got to the motel. He had just started down the dock toward the boat when he saw Megan running toward him. Even from the distance between them he knew something was wrong.

He started running, calling out as he ran, "What is it? What's the matter?"

"The bus." She slipped on the wet grass and fell to her knees.

He reached her and saw the tears, the fear. He lifted her to her feet. "What is it? What's happened?"

"There's been an accident. The school bus. A policeman called me."

"The school bus?" He grabbed her shoulders. "What did he say, Megan? What about Pilar?"

"I don't know," she sobbed. "He said..." She clutched his shoulders. "He said the bus had rolled over. I have to go to the hospital. I have to—"

"We'll go together."

She grabbed his hand and together they ran around the motel to her car. "I'll drive," he said. "You tell me where."

"Plantation Key. The Mariner's Hospital there."

"How far?"

"Fifteen miles."

Ricardo pulled onto the overseas highway and pressed the accelerator to the floor.

"If anything happens to her—" Megan started to say.

"Don't say that. Don't even think it! She's going to be all right, Megan. She has to be." He covered Megan's hand with his. "She has to be."

A mile farther down the highway they saw the bus. It was on its side, fifty feet off the road. There were black tire tracks where it had skidded. The front of it was smashed, the windows broken. Cars had stopped behind and in front and people were standing in the rain. Some of them were weeping.

Ricardo slowed. *"Por Dios,"* he said under his breath. He took Megan's hand again and squeezed it hard.

He said every prayer he'd ever known, prayed to every saint whose name he'd ever heard. A litany of prayer. Let her be all right. Just let her be all right. Pilar. His daughter. His Pilar.

The parking lot at the hospital was filled with cars. He pulled into the last space left. Before he could turn off the ignition Megan was out of the car and running toward the emergency entrance. He slammed his door and ran after her, and they went into the hospital together. The lobby was filled with people, some of them crying; others, their voices raised, were crowded in front of the reception window.

"I demand that you tell me how my son is," one of them said.

"I want to see my child," another cried.

"I want to see a doctor."

"Won't somebody tell me how my little girl is?"

Ricardo pushed his way past them. "Pilar Montoya," he said to the woman at the window. "I'm her father. This is her mother."

"I'm sorry, sir," the gray-haired woman at the window answered. "I don't have any information yet. I'm trying to tell people that. We're short-staffed here, but we're getting doctors and nurses coptered in from Marathon and Miami. Please sit down. We'll let you know just as soon as we can."

He tightened his hand around Megan's. It was clammy and cold. He looked at her and saw that her face was grayish-white. He put his arm around her shoulders. "Take it easy, Meggie."

"Pilar...I want to see her. I want—"

"I know, dear. And you will. We both will just as soon as they sort things out. It will take a little while, but somebody will come and tell us...." He gestured to the other parents and relatives milling around the room. "They'll tell all of us just as soon as they can, Meggie."

He led her to a chair, bought her a cola out of a machine and made her drink some of it. A little color came back into her cheeks.

He tried to think of something to say that would help to ease the look of fear, but he couldn't. He put his arm around her and prayed, Please let Pilar be all right. Please God.

A doctor in green scrubs came into the waiting room. The room hushed, then everyone started to speak at once. The doctor held up his hands. "Please!" he said. The room grew quiet again. He looked at the assembled parents and cleared his throat. "We're taking care of the children just as quickly as we can. In a little while we'll have a list of their names and room numbers and you parents can see them. Many of the injuries are minor and some of the children are being released." He gazed around the room. "Are Mr. and Mrs. Reynard here?"

A mailman, one arm around his obviously pregnant wife, raised his hand. "We're the Reynards," he said.

"I wonder if I might speak to you in the corridor."

"Jim?" The woman clutched her husband's arm. "What is it, Jim? Why—?"

"Come on, honey." His face had gone as pale as hers.

The doctor opened the door to the hall. "This way," he said.

The mailman and his wife followed him. The door closed behind them. For a moment no one spoke. Parent looked at parent, then away.

A scream shattered the silence. "Dear God," a woman said.

Megan gripped Ricardo's arm. He didn't say anything. Instead he led her to a corner of the room and put his arms around her. With his hand against the back of her head he pressed her close. "It's going to be all right," he whispered. "Take it easy, Meggie."

"I'm so scared."

"I know, *querida*. So am I."

Megan clung to him. "I'm glad you're here, Ricardo. Pilar loves you so much. She..." She burrowed her head against his chest. "Don't let go."

"I won't, Meggie. I won't let go."

They stayed like that, holding each other, one with the other parents, yet separate and apart, a unit unto themselves, husband and wife, united by fear and by the love of their child.

Almost two hours went by before the nurse at the desk began calling out names: Mr. and Mrs. Swormstedt, Mrs. Marino, Mr. and Mrs. Benson, Mr. John Raftery, Mr. and Mrs. Montoya. Mr. and Mrs....

With Ricardo's arm tight around Megan's waist, they followed the other parents and a young nurse out of the waiting room and down a long corridor.

"The children have been placed four beds to a room," the nurse said. "I'll call out the names that are in each room. Some of the children have been medicated, so please go in quietly. A doctor or a nurse will come in as soon as they can to tell you your child's condition."

She paused before the first room and called out four names. The parents, their faces strained and anxious, went in quickly.

Pilar's name was listed in the third room.

Ricardo and Megan went in, along with the other parents. There were two beds on each side of the room. Pilar was in the last bed on the right, next to a boy with red hair and freckles. Her eyes were closed. There was a bandage around her head and a long, angry scratch on her cheek. Her left arm was in a cast.

Megan gasped. With Ricardo's arm still around her waist they hurried to the bed. "Pilar?" she said softly. "It's Mama, honey."

Pilar's eyelids fluttered. "Mom?"

"Yes, baby." Megan sat on the edge of the bed and took Pilar's hand.

Pilar opened her eyes. "There was an accident. All the kids were screaming. It was terrible, Mom."

"I know it was, baby. But you're safe now."

"My head hurts." She saw Ricardo. "Dad? Dad?"

"I'm right here, *muchachita*."

"Don't leave. Okay?"

"I won't, Pilar." He knelt beside the bed and took her other hand.

"But tomorrow... you're gonna leave tomorrow."

Ricardo shook her head. "I won't go. I won't leave you." He tucked her small hand into his. "I'll stay just as long as you want me to."

A small smile tugged at the corners of her mouth. "Forever," she murmured, and closed her eyes. "Forever."

Chapter 9

Dr. Benjamin Weiss, a thin man with a receding hairline and black horn-rimmed glasses, met with them in the corridor outside the room three hours after Pilar had been admitted. An internist with a large practice in Miami, he looked, as far as Ricardo was concerned, too young to be a doctor.

"Your daughter has had a nasty bump on her head and she has a concussion," he said. "I'm not sure how severe it is right now, but I have given word that I want her monitored every hour. The bruises and the scratches are superficial. Her left arm was broken and it's been set. The cast can come off in five weeks."

"How long will she have to stay in the hospital?" Megan asked.

"It depends on the concussion. I'd say three or four days."

"Can we stay with her?" Ricardo asked.

"Usually I'd say no, but in the case of children this age I think it's a good idea for a parent to stay. But only one at a time. The two of you can work it out." He looked at Megan, noticed her pallor and said, "You look pretty done in, Mrs. Montoya. Why don't you get some rest tonight and let your husband stay with your daughter?"

"But I—" Megan started to protest.

"We'll do it any way you want to." Ricardo put his arm around her, then asked, "What about the other children, Doctor?"

"We've got a lot of broken bones and some bad cuts, but most of the children will be able to go home in a day or two." He took his glasses off and pinched the skin between his eyebrows. "We lost one. That was hard. And the little Benson boy has internal injuries as well as a concussion. We're keeping our fingers crossed."

"Benson?" Ricardo asked. "Willie Bob Benson?"

Weiss nodded. "Do you know him?"

"No, but he's a friend of my daughter's. That's him in the bed next to hers, isn't it?"

Weiss nodded. "Poor little guy. His mother's down sick with the flu and his father is somewhere on a ship in the South Pacific." He put a hand on Megan's shoulder. "Your daughter is going to be all right, Mrs. Montoya. Try not to worry."

When he left, they went back into the room. Pilar was asleep. Ricardo didn't want to go, but he knew how badly Megan needed to be with her now. "I'll be down in the waiting room. If you need anything let me know."

Megan took his hand. "Thank you for being here, Ricardo. Please . . . don't leave tomorrow."

"I won't, Meggie. I'll be here for as long as you and Pilar need me."

"We need you," she said.

He went back down the hall to the waiting room. As soon as he walked in, Tyrone, who had been standing by the door, hurried over to him.

"I heard about the accident on the radio after you and Miss Megan went runnin' to her car," Tyrone said. "Terrible thing. All those children. How's the little girl?"

"She's got a concussion and a broken arm, but we're pretty sure she's going to be all right."

"Lord, Lord." Tyrone worried his hands along the old straw hat. "How's Miss Megan doin'?"

"She was pretty badly shaken up, Tyrone, but she's got it under control. The doctor said only one of us could be with Pilar at a time, so Megan's with her now. I hope I can convince her to go back to the motel tonight."

"It's goin' to be mighty hard gettin' her away from Pilar. Those two purely dote on each other. Never seen anythin' like it. Miss Megan just worships that girl. If anythin' happened—" Tyrone shook his head. "I don't reckon you'll be leavin' in the morning?"

"No, I won't leave."

"That's good. Miss Megan will be needin' you, and so will little Pilar. Is it all right if I sit here a spell with you?"

"I'd like it if you would."

"I don't guess nobody but kin can see the child."

"I'm afraid not."

"I could tell 'em I'm her grandpappy, but I don't reckon they'd believe me, me being the wrong color, I mean."

For the first time that afternoon Ricardo smiled. "As soon as Pilar's better, I'll make sure you see her." He clamped a hand on Tyrone's knee. "We'll tell them you're her uncle, her grandfather or her third cousin. But we'll get you in."

People came and went all that long afternoon, harried parents who had just learned of the bus accident, a father whose son was in surgery, a worried grandmother watching two small children while her daughter was at the bedside of her other daughter. When darkness came, Ricardo said, "I'm going to try to get Megan to go out for dinner."

"Then I'll be moseyin' along." Tyrone picked up his straw hat from the seat next to him.

"No, you come to dinner with us," Ricardo said. "Wait here while I go up and get Megan."

But it was hard trying to convince her to leave Pilar. "I don't want any dinner," she protested. "I want to stay here."

"But you haven't eaten since noon," Ricardo argued. "We'll have dinner, then Tyrone will take you home and I'll come back and stay with Pilar."

"But I'm her mother."

"And I'm her father." Ricardo hesitated. "I've done so little for her, Megan. Please let me do this."

She caught her lower lip between her even white teeth, torn between telling him that this was her daughter and she had more right than he did to be here. For the past five years she had made every decision, taken every responsibility and faced every crisis alone. Now Ricardo was here, and he wanted to help because he, too, loved Pilar. She understood that, but it was hard to step back and accept the help he offered.

The nurse who had just given the young Benson boy an injection said, "You folks go on out and have something to eat. I'm going to be checking on the boy every thirty or forty minutes, and I'll check on your daughter, too. She's sleeping, and I doubt if she'll awaken before morning."

Ricardo thanked her, and with an arm firmly around Megan's waist, he led her from the room.

The three of them went to a fish place right on the water that Tyrone knew. Megan insisted she wasn't hungry, but Ricardo managed to get her to drink a glass of wine and eat half a bowl of fish chowder.

"I want you to go back to the motel with Tyrone," he told her when they left the restaurant. And when she started to object, he said, "Pilar will probably sleep through the night like the nurse said. I'll stay with her, and if there's any change, I'll call you."

"Mr. Ricardo's right, Miss Megan," Tyrone put in. "Won't do that little girl no good to see her mama lookin' so upset."

At last Megan gave in. "You'll call me if there's any change?" she said when Ricardo helped her into the pickup.

"Of course, I will." He kissed her cheek. "Take your time in the morning. I'm not going anywhere."

"Thank God," she said softly, and for a moment her gaze lingered on his in a silent communication. There was so much she wanted to say. She wanted to tell him how deep-down grateful she was that he was here and that she didn't know how she could have coped with this without him. She knew this was as difficult for him as it was for her, and that he loved their daughter as much as she did. She wanted to tell him, too, that she needed him, that she'd needed him all the long years they had been apart. And so had Pilar. But because she couldn't say all those things, Megan reached for his hand and said, "I'll see you in the morning, Ricardo."

He put his arms around her and held her for a moment. Then he let her go.

The hospital was quiet when he went back down the corridor to Pilar's room. There was a dim light near the canvas-backed chair in a corner, as well as a light over Willie Bob's bed. All of the children were sleeping.

Ricardo picked the chair up and took it over to Pilar's bed. She stirred for a moment and he whispered, "Go back to sleep, *niña*. Daddy's here." He took her hand, and though she didn't open her eyes, her fingers curled around his.

In the faint light above the bed he studied her face. With her eyes closed and her fair hair tumbled around her face she looked as he imagined Megan must have looked at her age. She was a slender, small-boned child, and he thought that in a few years she would grow to be taller than Megan. He smiled at the cleft in her chin, pleased because it was, like her amber eyes, from him, sweet proof of the love he and her mother had shared, a beautiful combination of Megan's Irish and English background and of his Spanish, Indian and Mexican blood. She was the best of both of them, and he loved her unconditionally with his heart and soul.

Let other men brag of their sons. She was his daughter, and he wouldn't have changed her for a dozen sons.

He thought back to the spring night in Granada when she was conceived. He and Megan had taken rooms in a small hotel near the Alhambra, and that early evening they had walked through the beautiful gardens there. The mimosa was in bloom, jasmine scented the air. He had kissed her there in the moonlight. "I want to make love with you," he'd said.

She'd looked up at him, and it had seemed to him that he'd never seen anyone as beautiful as she was. The stars were reflected in her eyes, the moon had turned her pale hair to gold.

She had put her arms around him. "Oh, yes," she'd said. "Let's hurry back to the hotel, Ricardo."

They had undressed each other in the darkened room, letting their clothes fall where they would, so anxious were they for the sweet coupling, touching each other, sharing long, moist kisses, whispering words of love. And when their bodies joined, she had said, as she did each time they loved, "Oh, yes, like that. Oh, darling. Darling."

And later, when they lay side by side in the moon-shadowed room, she'd said, "I think you gave me a baby tonight, Ricardo."

She couldn't have known, yet somehow she had. And nine months to the day Pilar had been born. Of their love, of his and Meggie's love.

The boy in the next bed began to moan. "Mama?" he called out. "Where are you, Mama?"

Ricardo got up and went to his bed. "Take it easy, boy."

Willie Bob opened his eyes. "I want my mom," he murmured.

"She'll be here as soon as she can, *muchacho.* Go back to sleep now."

"My stomach hurts." His chin quivered. "I wanna go home."

"I know, William. I know." Ricardo smoothed the curly red hair back from Willie Bob's forehead. "I'm going to be here with Pilar tonight. Did you know she has the bed next to yours? I'll move my chair between the two of you, and that way whenever you wake up you'll know you're not alone."

"She's my girlfriend," he murmured. "But don't tell her, okay?"

"I won't." Ricardo smiled and moved the chair between the two beds so that he would be close if either child called out.

Pilar woke when the night nurse came in to check her. "Daddy?" she said.

"Yes, Pilar, I'm here."

"My arm hurts." She began to whimper. "It hurts so bad."

"I know, *niña.* I'm sorry." He turned to the nurse. "Can't you give her something?"

"I will if she doesn't go back to sleep. A break like that is always painful for the first couple of days. Let me know if she gets too uncomfortable." She patted Pilar's shoulder. "Try to go back to sleep."

"I can't. My arm hurts and my head aches." Pilar began to cry.

Ricardo looked helplessly up at the nurse, but she shook her head. Before she turned away, though, she whispered, "Try to get her to sleep."

He smoothed the tousled hair back from Pilar's forehead. "Shh," he soothed. "I know it hurts, Pilar, but it will be better tomorrow. Go to sleep, baby."

"Where's Mom?"

"She was tired, Pilar. I made her go home."

"Are you going to stay?"

"Of course."

"Don't leave."

"I won't." He stroked her hand and began to sing in a voice so soft that only she, and perhaps the boy in the next bed, could hear:

"*A la ruru, niña,*
A la ruru, ya.
Duermate, mi niña,
Duermate, mi bien.
Go to sleep, my little girl,
Go to sleep, my treasure."

And at last, her hand in his, she slept.

He was helping Pilar with her breakfast the next morning when Megan came in with a bouquet of daisies and a small overnight case.

"You look better." Megan hugged her. "How do you feel?"

"I've got a headache and my arm hurts." Pilar lowered her voice to a whisper. "Willie Bob's real sick, Mom. The nurses keep coming in and looking at him all the time."

Megan looked over at the boy, then at Ricardo. "Poor little boy," she whispered. "I hope his dad gets home soon."

"Yes, so do I." He stood up to give her the chair. "Did you get some sleep?"

"Enough." She resisted an urge to smooth her hand over his unshaven cheek. "Now it's your turn. You look as though you could use a good eight hours."

"Maybe." He flexed his shoulders. "I'll be back about five and we'll have an early dinner."

"If Pilar's all right."

"Pilar will be fine." He bent down and gave his daughter a kiss. "Be sure and finish your cream of wheat," he told her.

"It tastes like paste."

"But it's good for you." He kissed her again, then he rested his hand on Megan's shoulder. "I'll see you later."

After he was gone, Megan took a new toothbrush, a pair of pink-and-white Minnie Mouse pajamas and two books out of the overnight case. "When you feel better, you might like to read," she said to Pilar.

"Maybe." Pilar pushed the breakfast tray aside with her good hand. "I don't want any more of that. My arm hurts. I don't feel good." She looked at Megan with teary eyes. "Daddy sang to me last night."

"He did?"

"Real nice and soft. In Spanish. I like it when he speaks Spanish. It's sorta soothing, you know?"

"I know."

Oh, yes, I know.

Words whispered in the dark. "*Mi vida, mi amor, mi mujer,* my life, my love, my woman. *Para siempre.*" His woman, Ricardo's woman. But it hadn't been forever.

"I love him," Pilar said.

"I know you do, sweetie."

"I want him to stay with us forever."

"Pilar..." Megan shook her head. "Your dad lives in Mexico."

"We could live there. We could all live at the ranch together."

"You'll be at the ranch this summer, Pilar."

"But you won't be there. I want you there, too. I want all of us together."

There was nothing Megan could say, no words to explain why they couldn't live together and be a family again. And because she couldn't explain, Megan picked up one of the books she had brought and began to read aloud.

When her lunch came, Pilar didn't want to eat. Her arm hurt and she was weepy. At four that afternoon Megan went out into the hall and phoned Ricardo. "Maybe you could bring something she'd like," she told him. "A hamburger or a pizza. Maybe a chocolate shake."

He came a little after five, just as they wheeled in Pilar's dinner tray—liver, a boiled potato and broccoli.

"You can take that away," he told the aide who'd brought the tray. "I've brought my daughter's dinner."

The aide looked at the pizza box and the bag that contained the cheeseburger and chocolate shake. "Looks like you lucked out tonight, kiddo," she said.

Pilar smiled for the first time that day. "This is my dad."

Ricardo put the pizza on the nightstand. "What will it be, *muchacho?* Pizza or cheeseburger?"

"Pepperoni pizza?"

"Yes."

"I'll have one piece of pizza, then the cheeseburger. Can I have a sip of the chocolate shake?"

"You can have anything you want." He kissed her, then inserted the straw into the top of the shake and handed it to her. Motioning to the two other little girls in the room, he said, "Maybe you'd like to share the pizza with them."

"Sure," Pilar said. "We could give some to Willie Bob, too, except I don't think he's feeling very good."

"No, he isn't." Megan glanced at Ricardo. "His mother was here for a little while this afternoon. She said the navy's trying to get her husband back on emergency leave." Megan lowered her voice. "He's an awfully sick little boy."

"But he's going to get better, isn't he?" Pilar asked anxiously.

"Yes, I'm sure he is." Ricardo squeezed her good hand. "After you eat, do you mind if your mom and I go out for dinner?"

"Are you going to stay with me tonight?"

"*Por supuesto,* of course, I am."

"Then it's okay if you and Mom go out for dinner. Just so you come back."

He smiled across the bed at Megan. "I'll come back," he said.

Three days later Dr. Weiss said that Pilar could leave, but when Megan and Ricardo went to pick her up, she didn't want to go home.

"It's Willie Bob," she confided in a whisper. "Sometimes he wakes up at night and we talk. He sorta depends on me because there isn't anybody else. His mom's still sick. His father's supposed to come tomorrow and it'll be okay if I leave then."

"But I thought you were anxious to get home," Megan said.

"I am, Mom. I'll come tomorrow."

"I don't know, honey. The doctor has already said you're well enough to go home."

"I'll talk to Dr. Weiss," Ricardo said. "If he says it's all right to keep you here until tomorrow, then that's what we'll do. It's nice of you to want to be with Willie Bob.''

Pilar blushed. "I don't like him or anything," she whispered. "And as soon as he gets better I'll probably hate him again, but now . . ." She shrugged, then winced in pain and said, "Now I feel kinda sorry for him."

Megan looked across the bed at Ricardo. "I like our daughter. I think we'll keep her."

He went out to call the doctor, and when he returned, he said, "It's all set, Pilar. You can stay tonight. Your mom and I will take you home tomorrow."

She put her good arm up, and when he bent down, she squeezed his neck. "I'm okay now. You don't have to stay with me tonight."

"Are you sure?"

She said that she was and that it was okay if they went out to dinner if they'd come back and tell her good-night.

After they ate, they came back to the hospital. Pilar and the other two little girls were watching television, so they kissed her good-night and told her they'd see her in the morning.

"You must be dead for sleep," Megan said when they left the hospital.

Ricardo shook his head. "I've slept enough during the day." He helped her into the car and got behind the wheel. "It'll be good to have her home again."

"Oh, yes." Megan leaned her head back against the leather seat. "I'll have to fix something special for dinner tomorrow night."

"Mexican." He smiled. "Let's fix her a real Mexican dinner—enchiladas, guacamole and red snapper Veracruz style. Do you remember how to fix that?"

"I remember everything." She turned her head and looked out the window. The night was hot and humid, soft with the smell of salt marshes and the whisper of palm fronds and cicadas.

Ricardo switched the car radio on. Patsy Cline was singing about the man she'd loved who'd done her wrong. He changed the station, found Caribbean music and kept it on.

Megan turned on the seat so that she could look at him. "Will you go back to Mexico now that Pilar's better?"

"Not for a while. Not as long as she wants me here." He hesitated. "Not unless you want me to go."

"I don't want you to go. I mean...I mean, because of Pilar."

"I know what you mean." He turned off of A1A onto the road that led to the motel. When he pulled up in front of her apartment, he switched off the ignition. "I'd like to stay until her school is out and take her back to the ranch with me, but I won't if you don't want me to."

"You're welcome to stay as long as you want to, Ricardo. I know you love Pilar and that she loves you." She tried to make her voice noncommittal, friendly, but there was a part of her that wanted to cry, "I want you to stay because of me, too. I need you as much as she does. I need ..."

She opened the door and got out of the car. He came around to her side, took her arm and went up onto her porch with her. "I'd ask you to come in for coffee," she said. "But we're both tired."

Ricardo nodded. "What time do you want to go to the hospital tomorrow?"

"The doctor said he'd see Pilar at eleven. She can go home right after that."

"Then I'll see you at ten?"

"Ten's fine." She took a deep breath. "Good night, Ricardo. Thank you for everything."

He shook his head. "I wish things could have been different, Megan. For us, I mean."

"So do I."

He came a step closer. She looked tired. Her hair was pulled straight back off her face, and there were smudges of fatigue under her eyes. "You need to rest," he said, and put his arms around her.

For a moment she stiffened, then she sighed and let her head droop against his shoulder.

He held her, soothing her with his hands, and because he couldn't help himself, he asked, in a voice so low that he could barely hear it, "Is it too late for us, Meggie?"

She looked up at him. "I...I don't know," she whispered. "I—"

He stopped her words with a kiss and his mouth was warm against hers. He kissed her with passion and with hunger, for things past, for the now and the here, with a desire so strong that his body shook.

He worked his mouth back and forth over hers, tasting, nibbling, sucking her lower lip, sampling her tongue, growling low in his throat because the need to take her was strong. He felt her tremble and sway against him. He heard her murmurs of protest, of desire, of a longing so like his own.

He held her away and she looked up at him. Her eyes were heavy-lidded, her mouth swollen from his kisses. She took a shuddering breath and put her hand against his chest. "No," she whispered. "No."

"Meggie . . . ?"

"I . . . I can't think straight right now. I'm tired. I . . ."

He stepped away from her, made as though to reach out for her, then dropped his hands to his sides.

"I've never stopped loving you," he said. And before she could answer he turned away and ran down the steps.

Chapter 10

Megan pressed her fingertips against lips that tingled from his touch. Her body throbbed with heated hunger, and because she knew that if she didn't go in she would call him back, she turned and ran into the apartment. Once inside she threw her purse down on a chair, kicked her shoes off and headed for the bathroom where she stripped out of her clothes and got into the shower without bothering to adjust the water temperature.

Leaning her hands flat against the shower wall, she let the tepid water pour over her feverish body. But though it soothed, it didn't cool the heat that made her shake with a need akin to pain. She put the palms of her hands against her throbbing breasts, then held them up to the cascading water. But it didn't help. Nothing helped.

I won't think about him, she told herself when she got out of the shower. I don't want it to start all over again. I don't want... She stood back and looked at herself in the mirror above the sink—naked, wet blond hair dripping down onto her shoulders, face strained, needy eyes staring back at her. She looked at the untouched breasts, at the waist that no man's hands had encircled in such a long time, at the narrow hips and the long legs, legs that once had gripped his body to urge him closer. Closer...

With a cry Megan put her hands up to cover her eyes so that she wouldn't have to look at her unloved, untouched body.

At last she moved away from the mirror. She toweldried her hair and put on a clean white nightgown. Because she knew she couldn't sleep, she went to stand by the window and looked out toward the water.

The night was still except for the rustle of palms in the offshore breeze. The smell of night-blooming jasmine and of the gardenia bushes she had planted under her bedroom window drifted on the night air.

"Ricardo." His name, like a half-forgotten sigh, whispered in the darkness of her room. "Ricardo."

He came out of the shower, a towel wrapped around his waist. The boat moved and he stopped where he was, alert for the sound of footsteps. When he heard the soft pad of bare feet on the deck above, he hesitated, then cautiously and quietly started up the steps to the deck.

She was there, bathed in moonlight, her body outlined through the thin fabric of her gown.

"Meggie?" Her name whispered from his lips. "Meggie?"

She turned, one hand fluttering to her throat. She tried to speak, but no words came.

He felt the sudden tightening of his body, the quick hardness. He took a step toward her, and because he had to be sure, he asked, "Why have you come?"

"I couldn't sleep. I..." She shook her head, and the pale hair swung loose around her shoulders. "No," she murmured, "I came because I...because I—"

He took her hands in his. "Shh," he said, "it's all right. I know. Will you come below with me now?"

A sigh trembled through her. "It's been so long," she murmured. "There hasn't been anybody else, Ricardo. Not since you."

He let go of her hands so that he could put his arms around her, and there was a tightness in his throat, a constriction in his chest because she was so delicate, so incredibly fragile. He felt the tremors of her body, the smallness of her bones and the velvet smoothness of her skin beneath the thin protection of the white gown. He kissed the side of her face. "It will be all right. It will be good. It always was. That won't have changed."

He let her go and, taking her hand, led her down the steps to the cabin where the only light was the shaded glow above the bunk. "Raise your arms," he said, and when she did, he lifted the white gown over her head.

She was still as slender as the day he had met her; the tender curves were the same, the shade and shadow of body contour just as he remembered. Her breasts were high and round and full, the small blush peaks thrust forward, waiting for his touch.

He tugged at the towel that covered him from waist to thigh and let it drop, and when he heard the catch of breath in her throat, he put his hands on her shoulders and drew her close. Though her skin was cool, he could feel the heat in her, the almost indiscernible thrum of a body tense and waiting. He breathed in the faint scent of a woman ready for love and took her warm, moist mouth.

She moaned low in her throat and began to move against him. He cupped her bottom and brought her closer. Hot blood rushed to his loins, and he swelled against her, burning with need. It was all he could do not to take her here, standing.

He held her away from him, straining for control, his eyes narrowed with desire. "Come," he said in a voice made hoarse by all he was feeling. He drew her down to the bunk and held her in his arms. "It's been so long," he whispered against her throat. He touched her breasts, as tenderly, as tentatively as he had that first time so long ago. He'd been afraid then that she would pull away. But now, as then, she didn't.

Instead she put her hands against his face and said, "Oh, yes. Oh, please, yes."

With trembling fingers she outlined the open mouth that suckled her breasts, traced the curve of his ears and moved down over his shoulders and the corded muscles of his back, down over the smooth line of his hips.

She had almost forgotten how good this could be, how tender was his mouth, how the touch of his hands on her body could excite her.

He smoothed his hands across her stomach, down to the apex of her legs, and began to stroke her there. She pressed her head against his shoulder and sighed with pleasure.

"Is it all right?" she whispered. "I mean, because you were hurt? Will it hurt you if we...if we do this?"

"It will hurt me if we don't." He kissed her. "I need you, Meggie," he whispered. "I need you so."

She sighed against his lips and began to stroke him as he stroked her.

He gasped. His big body stretched and strained. He found her mouth and kissed her, deep and hard, with all the pent-up longing he'd felt from the moment she'd walked back into his life. He wanted to wait, to savor this light and gentle touching. But he couldn't, and with a strangled cry he rolled her beneath him and quickly, almost violently, thrust into her hot and ready moistness.

Shock surged through Megan, and for the barest fraction of a moment she tried to pull back. It had been so long, five years since he had touched her this way. "Wait," she whispered. "I..." But suddenly, suddenly it was all right, it was the way it had always been between them. Their bodies fitted so perfectly that it was as though they had been designed for each other, for this one perfect act.

He moved deeply into her and her body welcomed him. He took her mouth, and her lips parted under his and she lifted herself to him, moving as he moved, their bodies in perfect harmony, heartbeat against heartbeat, rising, falling, coming closer and closer to that final moment.

He stroked deep and hard, withdrew and thrust again. "Look at me, Meggie-love," he whispered. "Look at me now."

Her body caught fire, yearning, straining, and he held her there, held her on the precipice of passion.

"Oh, yes!" he cried. "Oh, yes!" And then it happened, for her and for him, and when she cried out, he took her cry and made it his own.

Megan clung to him, whimpering with pleasure as wave after wave of ecstasy trembled through her, holding him as he held her, one with him, a part of him, flesh of his flesh.

He rained kisses on her face, her closed eyelids, her mouth. He couldn't stop kissing her, couldn't get close enough to her because she was here at last as he had dreamed she might one day be. He held her close because there was a part of him still afraid that this might be a dream, that she would vanish as quickly as she had come. If he kept her a prisoner of his arms, she wouldn't be able to leave him. If this was a dream, he would cling to it as long as he could.

But it wasn't a dream. Megan was here, holding him as he held her, stroking his shoulders and his back, whispering small love words, telling him how he had pleased her, how he made her feel. Sigh after sigh of pure contentment escaping her lips, she purred low in her throat and snuggled closer.

"I'd forgotten how good this was between us," she said. "How being with you could make me feel."

Ricardo smoothed the tumbled hair back off her face. "There hasn't been anybody else?" he asked. "*¿Te veras?* Truly?"

"No one. Not after you, Ricardo. Never anyone but you."

He had been her first, and though he knew it was an arrogant macho attitude, his heart swelled because there hadn't been anyone else for her, even after all these years.

He wanted to tell her there hadn't been anyone for him, either, but he couldn't. For there had been, casual women, casual affairs to assuage the loneliness because Meggie had left him, because she hadn't wanted him. But in a strange way there really hadn't been another woman in his life, because after each affair he had been left with a sadness of heart, an un-satisfied emptiness because none of them had been Megan. With none of them had he shared what he had just experienced with her.

"Tell me why you came to me tonight, Meggie," he said. She lifted her face, and in the dim light he touched the lips still swollen from his kisses. "Tell me."

Megan rested her head against his shoulder, one arm around his waist. "I wanted to be close to you to-night, Ricardo." She kissed his shoulder. "I wanted it to be like it was before."

He rubbed his chin back and forth across her hair. "I never stopped wanting you. I never will."

Nor I you, she wanted to say, but even now, after what they had shared, it was hard to let go, to surren-der to everything she felt, to the bittersweet knowl-edge that she still loved him.

They rested, half sleeping, half waking, and in a little while she said, "I should go back to the apart-ment."

"No, stay with me tonight."

"But somebody might see me, in the morning, I mean. Tyrone—"

"Will understand." He kissed the top of her head. "You won't be able to stay after Pilar comes home, so stay tonight. I want to sleep with you beside me, Me-gan. I want to make love to you again. I don't want to let you go. Not yet. Not ever."

"No promises," she whispered. "It's too soon." She turned her head into his shoulder. "I'll stay to-night, though. We'll sleep together and we..." She curled her fingers through his chest hair. "We'll do whatever you want to do, Ricardo."

It began again, the hot zing of excitement, the surge of warmth in his loins. She caressed his chest and followed the line of hair that curled down from his navel. And when he made as though to gather her in his arms, she said, "I want to touch you like this," and she began to caress him, to fondle and tease with the soft scrape of her fingernails, and all the while she trailed soft kisses across his shoulders and his chest.

He gasped with pleasure against her lips, and when she murmured, "Oh, Ricardo," he knew he couldn't wait. Grasping the hand that had so sweetly tortured, he took it and the other to raise above her head.

Her breasts in the faint light were so beautiful that they took away his breath. He began to kiss them, moving closer to the rosy peaks, and though she moaned and tried to free her hands, he wouldn't let her go. A thrill of excitement, unlike anything he had ever known, shivered through him. Still holding her a prisoner, he took one peak between his teeth to tug and squeeze, to lap and suckle.

Her body began to writhe. She whispered his name, and he thought he would die with wanting her. But still he made her wait, as he waited, for that sweet, hot moment when their bodies would become one. And then she said, "Oh, please, now, please. I can't stand it, please." So he let go of her wrists and took her mouth and kissed her long and deep and hard, and with a low cry he entered her.

She whispered incoherent words of passion and held him with her arms and with smooth, long legs that wrapped around his back.

He moved with exquisite slowness, holding her there, gentling her, making her wait because he wanted it to last. He ground his body against hers, withdrew and plunged again, harder, deeper.

Every nerve was sensitive, aware, tingling with an intense pleasure that left her breathless. How could she have forgotten how good this was? She wanted it to go on and on. She didn't want him ever to stop.

"Ah, love," he whispered against her lips. "So good, my Meggie. So good."

She kissed his shoulder. "I love what you do to me," she said, and put her hands against the small of his back to hold him there. And because she couldn't help herself she said, "I love you, Ricardo. I've never stopped loving you."

Tears stung her eyes, and when they fell, he lapped them with his tongue. "Don't cry, my Meggie-girl. Don't cry, my little love."

And his heart swelled with a tenderness unlike anything he had ever known, for this was his Meggie and she loved him. After all the old bitterness, after all the years apart, she could still say the words he so longed to hear. He didn't know how it would end for them, but for now, for this time, she was his again.

He moved more gently now, and if anything, that very gentleness was even more exciting than that first fierce coupling. Like waves at high tide that build higher and higher as they near the shore, surging deep and rolling up from the ocean depth, so came her passion, swelling from deep inside her, growing, growing until it was past bearing and her body soared and broke and burst with an intensity that left her shaking and breathless.

He took her cry and held her so close that she could barely breathe while his own storm of passion burst and broke and he collapsed over her.

They lay for a long time without speaking, still joined as one, and when he made as though to move from her, she said, "No, don't leave me yet."

"I'm too heavy for you."

"No, stay. I love the feel of you over me." She pressed him closer. "In me."

"All right," he said. "We'll stay like this. We'll sleep like this."

Megan closed her eyes. He whispered, "Sleep with the angels, my love," and though she didn't think she would, she went immediately to sleep.

She awakened, shifted and stretched, and slept again, always aware of his body on hers, of that essence of him still joined to her. The passion they had shared had ebbed but hadn't gone away. Each time he moved against her the sensation was there. Half awake and half asleep, she sighed against his lips and tightened the muscles that would hold him there.

In the first soft light of morning, with the slight rock of the boat on the morning tide, she felt his quiet shifting, felt him grow and swell. Without opening her eyes she began to stroke his shoulders and to nuzzle her face against his throat.

"Nice," she murmured. "Nice."

They made love again, slowly, quietly, and in that final moment he murmured words in Spanish that she didn't understand but loved to hear, gentle words of love and passion. Spent, he turned with her so that he could cradle her in his arms, and kiss her eyes, her cheeks and mouth, and tell her, now in English, how dear and precious she was, how much he needed her.

The next time she awoke Ricardo was sitting on the edge of the bed with a steaming hot cup of coffee in his hand.

"It's eight-thirty," he said.

"Eight!" She sat up. "We have to get to the hospital."

"They won't release Pilar until eleven. There's plenty of time." She looked very pretty this morning, tousled and well loved, fair hair streaming around her shoulders, the sheet pulled up over her breasts to cover her nakedness. He handed her the cup and said, "Drink it while I fix breakfast."

She accepted the cup, sniffed the coffee and took a tentative sip. "Wonderful. I may possibly survive, after all." A smile curved the corners of her mouth. "You know you've ruined me, don't you? And that I may never walk properly again."

He laughed because he had forgotten that for all of her ladylike manner and her occasional shyness she could once in a while surprise him with a touch of bawdiness that he found delightful. It pleased him that that hadn't changed, that she hadn't changed.

He tugged the sheet down, cupped her breasts in both of his hands and ran his thumbs across the suddenly peaked nipples.

Her eyes widened. "You're kidding!"

"Yes." He laughed and got up. "Breakfast in fifteen minutes. I found a pair of your shorts and a shirt in one of the storage closets. I hung them in the bathroom."

"Thank you, Ricardo," she said, and when he turned to go into the galley, she leaned back against the pillows and sipped her coffee. She was tired, but it was a good tiredness. All of the tension of these past weeks, and of the terrible few days since the bus accident, had vanished. Her body felt light and clean and free. And loved. Oh, yes, loved.

She wasn't sure, in the cool, clear light of the morning, how she felt about that. She tried to tell herself that she should be thinking seriously about what had happened last night, about what it all meant, about the repercussions of their having made love again after all these years. But all she could do was smile.

At last she went in to shower and dress, and when she went out into the galley, she saw that Ricardo had set the table with tall glasses of orange juice and sliced mangoes and papaya, and that he had just finished frying bacon and scrambling eggs.

"Do you actually think we're going to eat all this food?" she asked.

"¡Cómo no, mujer!" He grinned and kissed her. "After last night we need food for energy. And strength for tonight."

"Not tonight," Megan said. "Pilar will be home."

"And you must be with her. Of course." Ricardo nodded. "But when she's better, when she's at school, we'll be together as we were last night. Yes?"

"Ricardo, I..." Megan shook her head. "I don't know if we should." She reached across the table and took his hand. "I'm not having second thoughts about last night. It was heaven being with you again."

"Then why?" He raised one eyebrow. "I don't understand, Meggie. What are you saying? That we must never make love again?"

"No, not that. But I think...I think we should go cautiously, Ricardo. We can't just think about ourselves. We have to consider Pilar. She's grown so close to you in these past few weeks. She loves you."

"And I love her." He tightened his hand around Megan's. "I don't understand. What are you saying?"

"That in spite of last night nothing's really changed, between us, I mean." She looked down at the strong bronzed hand holding hers. "The reason we separated hasn't changed."

"You were little more than a child when we married. You didn't understand my profession, or that it's part of who I am."

"I'm not sure I understand now, Ricardo."

"We can work it out," he said. "I'm older. I'll be more understanding of the way you feel. I'm still passionate about what I do—that hasn't changed—but I'm not as hot-blooded as I once was."

"Aren't you?"

He grinned, understanding her meaning. "Only with you. When I'm with you, my blood is as hot as it was when I was a teenager. I wish I'd known you then. I wish I'd spent every day of my life with you." He leaned across the table, and in an impassioned voice he said, "I wish now that I'd refused to let you leave me. I wish I'd locked you in a room and kept you there, because I've hated every moment we've been apart, every night we haven't made love, every morning I've awakened without you beside me."

"Ricardo—"

"I won't let you go again," he said. "Not after last night. You said you loved me, Meggie. How can I let you go again after that?" He brought her hand to his lips and kissed it. "Now eat your breakfast. Soon it will be time to leave for the hospital."

After they ate, Megan kissed Ricardo, then she jumped off the boat and started down the dock. But she stopped when she saw Tyrone on the deck of the charter boat.

"Mornin', Miss Megan," he called out. "It surely is a pretty day, isn't it? You fixin' to fetch Pilar from the hospital?"

"Yes. I . . . I just went down to the . . . to the sailboat to . . . ah, to make sure Ricardo was almost ready. I mean, in case he wanted to come with me."

"Yes, ma'am."

"I . . . I'd better hurry. I mean, I have to change my clothes. I put these on to . . . to tell Ricardo . . ."

Tyrone smiled. "If you don't mind me sayin' so, Miss Megan, dressed up or not, you surely are as pretty as a picture this morning."

She blushed. "Thank . . . thank you, Tyrone. I'd better—"

"Yes, ma'am. You hurry along now."

When she turned and ran toward the apartment, he grinned and shook his head. "Now don't that beat all. Don't that just beat all."

Chapter 11

The days that followed were some of the happiest, and at the same time some of the most troubled, Megan had ever known. She thought she had forgotten what it had been like making love with Ricardo, but she hadn't. Every memory of the way it had been came flooding back, and she wanted to weep for all of the years away from him, for all of the nights they hadn't shared.

They had only managed to be together twice since Pilar had come home. Both those times had been hurried and unsatisfying because she had worried that Agnes or one of the guests might need her, that Tyrone had seen her go aboard the *Sea Chum* and disappear below, or that Pilar—for whatever reason—might come home from school early. Rather than assuage her hunger, their brief lovemaking only confused her. She wanted and needed to be with Ricardo, but still she was afraid of letting her emotions get the best of her, of being hurt again.

It was a joy to have Pilar safely home. In spite of her broken arm she was just as lively and happy as she had always been. She was back in school, but instead of riding the bus Ricardo drove her back and forth.

"She isn't going to get on one of those run-down school buses ever again," he'd said the night before Pilar had returned to school. "From now on I'll drive her."

Though Pilar protested, Megan sensed she was secretly pleased that Ricardo had assumed his role as her father and that he was taking care of her. And while Megan hadn't been happy about having Pilar ride the new school bus the county had provided, that actually wasn't new at all but even more dilapidated and run-down than the bus that had had the accident, she resented Ricardo's interference. He hadn't been a part of Pilar's life for five years, but now that he was here he was taking over. He was making the decisions. And though she tried not to, she felt a twinge of jealousy because Pilar had acceded so readily to his wishes, that she looked to him to make decisions for her rather than to her mother.

He had dinner with them every evening, sometimes at the apartment, and sometimes the three of them went to a restaurant. And each night when it was time to say good-night, he kissed both mother and daughter.

The first time he kissed Megan, Pilar's mouth had fallen open before she covered it with her hand and tried to smother a delighted giggle. As soon as they were inside, she said, "Daddy kissed you!"

"Well . . . yes."

"And you sorta kissed him back."

Megan smiled. "Sorta."

"Do you like each other again? Are you going to get married?"

"We never stopped being married, Pilar. Your dad and I just decided not to live together."

"But if you're kissing, doesn't that mean you're going to be like married people again?"

Like married people who lived together and made love together. Megan clenched her hands to her sides so that Pilar wouldn't see their sudden trembling.

"Where will we live, Mom? Here or in Mexico? It's okay with me if we live in Mexico, but I'm not sure my Spanish is good enough to go to school there. Do you think it is? I wonder what the school will be like."

"Whoa!" Megan said. "Slow down! Your dad and I are friends, Pilar, but we haven't talked about getting back together."

"But you like each other."

"Yes," Megan said. "We like each other, but..." She hesitated. "Maybe you shouldn't say anything about this to your dad."

"About the kissing?" Pilar nodded. "Okay, I won't say anything about kissing."

But the next morning on the way to school she asked, "You still like Mom, don't you, Dad?"

"Of course, I like her."

"Do you love her?"

He hadn't expected this. He'd known, of course, that Pilar had been watching both him and her mother with obvious curiosity, and now he realized she'd like nothing better than to see him and Megan back together again.

He wasn't sure how he felt about that. His and Meggie's marriage hadn't worked the first time, and though they were both more mature now, the problems that had separated them remained the same. He still loved her—that hadn't changed. She was a beautiful and desirable woman, but as for their getting back together again—he wasn't sure how he felt about that. He needed more time.

"Some of my friends asked me about you and Mom. I told them you aren't really married anymore, and yesterday José Fernandez said something I didn't understand, about you and Mom living here together, and Willie Bob punched him in the nose."

Ricardo tightened his hands around the steering wheel. This was something he hadn't thought about, that people, especially Pilar's friends, might be gossiping about him and Megan. He didn't mind for himself, but Megan was in the tourist business, and that kind of talk wouldn't be good for her. Certainly it wasn't good for Pilar.

But because he wasn't sure how to handle Pilar's questions, he asked, "How *is* Willie Bob?"

"He's better, but he's still sorta pale. I think Miss Royce would have really punished him yesterday if he hadn't just gotten out of the hospital."

Ricardo stopped in front of the school. "I'll see you at three," he said, thinking he had diverted her attention from the subject of he and Megan.

But he hadn't. "I wouldn't mind living in Mexico," she said. "If you and Mom got unseparated, I mean. I like Grandma and Aunt Isabel. Grandpa's kind of grouchy, but I like him okay."

Before he could answer she hugged him with her good arm and hopped out of the car. "See ya," she called over her shoulder.

Ricardo thought about his conversation with Pilar all that day, and he decided that when he picked her up later he would talk to her about it. But that afternoon, before he could say anything, she hopped into the car and said, "I've got a letter for you and Mom from my teacher."

"*¿Porqué?* Why?" He smiled, and though he couldn't imagine it, he asked, "Did you do something wrong?"

"Of course not," Pilar said indignantly. "This is about an outing."

"An outing? I don't understand, Pilar. What's that?"

"It's when a bunch of kids and some teachers go away on a special class trip. We're going to Key West."

"Without your parents?"

Pilar nodded. "It's just for the second and third grades, and this is a letter for Mom to sign saying I can go."

Ricardo shook his head. "I'm not sure that's a good idea. Your arm is still in the cast and—"

"But I want to go," she wailed. "All the other kids are going. We're going to see the turtle kraals and the museum and the aquarium and go out in a glass-bottomed boat. Please, Dad. It'll be a real adventure."

"You'll have to ask your mother," he said. "But I don't think so, Pilar."

When they did ask her, Megan said the same thing he had said. "I don't think it's a good idea, Pilar, not while your arm's still in a cast."

"But all the kids are going!"

"You don't know that, honey. Besides, you're not just any kid. You're my kid, and I don't think I want you to go."

"But, Mom—"

The phone in the kitchen interrupted the rest of what Pilar was going to say. When Megan hurried out of the room to answer it, Pilar turned to Ricardo. "Can't you convince her, Dad?" she whispered.

"I'm afraid I agree with your mother, Pilar. I don't like the idea of your going away without one of us with you." He put his arm around her. "I'm sorry, *muchacha*. I . . ." He looked up as Megan came back into the room.

"That was Mrs. Benson," she said, "Willie Bob's mother. She's going along on the trip and so are Betsy Ball's and little Dottie Tulp's mothers. She's promised to look after Pilar."

Ricardo shook his head. "I don't think—"

"Dad, please!"

He looked over at Megan.

"Most of the other children are going," she said.

"For how many days?"

"They'd leave Friday noon and be back Sunday before dark."

"On the school bus?"

"No. The parents and teachers will be driving."

"*Pues* . . . if you think it's all right . . ."

"Mom, *please!*"

"Okay," Megan said. "But you promise—"

"Anything!"

On Friday morning Pilar kissed Megan good-bye and got into the car with Ricardo. She was dressed in blue jeans, a new red-and-white-striped T-shirt and new red sneakers. She chattered like a seven-year-old magpie all the way to school, and when they arrived, she hugged Ricardo and said, "Thank you a million times for letting me go, Dad."

"Have a good time, Pilar, but be careful of your arm."

"I will." She kissed him, and then she was out of the car, running toward the school, braid flying out behind her, off on a real adventure. And Ricardo smiled because she was his and because he loved her.

Megan was working in the little office off the reception room that afternoon when Ricardo knocked on the door and went in.

"Get your gear together," he said. "The *Sea Chum* leaves in exactly forty-five minutes."

She looked up from the papers she'd been working on. "I can't leave. There's too much to do."

"Agnes has agreed to work this weekend. All of the rooms and the efficiencies are filled. Tyrone has a charter tomorrow morning, but the rest of the time he'll stand by in case Agnes needs anything."

"But I can't just—"

"Yes, you can." He glanced at his watch. "Forty-two minutes."

"But—"

"Forty-one." He pulled her up out of the chair. "The boat is stocked and ready to go. I'll give you time to change and pack whatever you want to take for the weekend, but I'm warning you, if you're not ready..." He looked at his watch again. "If you're not ready in exactly forty minutes, you'll go with what you're wearing." He took a step closer. "Because you're going if I have to shanghai you. Understand?''

Megan faced him, hands on her hips, not quite sure whether to be amused or angry by his highhandedness. Through the closed office door she could hear Agnes typing.

"Thirty-nine minutes," he said.

"All right!" She frowned up at him. "Where are we going?"

He cupped the back of her neck with his hand and drew her slowly toward him. "Does it matter?"

Something gave way inside her, and a hot trickle of flame licked through her.

"Two days and two nights," Ricardo whispered. "Say yes, Meggie."

She felt as though her legs wouldn't support her. He tightened his hold on the back of her neck, and she swayed toward him.

"Our time," he said against her lips. "Our loving time." And before she could move away his mouth took hers. His breath was hot, his lips firm, insistent, demanding.

Megan clung to him, hands curled against his blue denim shirt, her hungry mouth moving against his. From out of the past came the memory of the first time she had seen him, and how she had thought how wickedly full his lips were. And they were, full and ripe, tantalizing and warm, both giving and demanding.

He drew her closer, one hand against the small of her back. Like her, he was wearing shorts. His legs were strong and hard against hers. She felt the press of his body, and a half-smothered moan escaped her lips.

Abruptly he let her go and held her away from him. His eyes were hooded with passion, his nostrils flared. "If you're not down at the boat in exactly thirty minutes, I'm coming back for you," he muttered. "I'll lock the door and take you right here on the floor." He gripped her shoulders. "You've got a choice, Meggie. Here or the boat?"

She stood on tiptoe and wound her arms around his neck. "We'd better not shock Miss Agnes," she said a little breathlessly, and before he could answer she turned and ran out of the room.

There had never been a more beautiful sunset. The sky was paintbrush perfect, an artist's dream of flamingo-pink, gold and green and blue that stretched for miles on the horizon of the water. They were in the bow of the boat, anchored in a sheltered cove near Tavernier, drifting slowly on the ebb tide. The only sound was the splash of waves against the hull, the cry of the gulls, and of the great white heron and the sandhill cranes that came to feed in the shallows of the cove.

"I like Florida," Ricardo said. "I'll miss it when I leave."

Don't leave, she wanted to say. But didn't.

He had chilled a bottle of champagne and had fixed small plates of appetizers—caviar, smoked salmon, cream cheese, crackers and crisp rounds of black bread.

He hadn't touched her since they had come aboard. She knew what the waiting cost him; it was in his eyes when he touched his glass to hers, in the deep huskiness of his voice when he spoke.

"I bought steaks for dinner," he said. "But I thought we could eat later, if that's all right with you."

Megan nodded. "Later is fine." She spread a bit of cream cheese on a crispy round and added a piece of salmon.

A fish jumped and splashed near the boat.

"I wonder what Pilar's doing now," she said.

"Pretending to fight with Willie Bob." Ricardo added more champagne to her glass, then put a dab of caviar on a cracker and held it up to her mouth. When she took it, his fingers lingered on her lips, but only for a moment.

Megan looked at him over the rim of her glass. The fire that had warmed her body when he kissed her in the office flared again at his touch. He raised his glass and she saw his hand tremble.

Soon, she thought. Soon.

But still he waited, waited until the moon, full and fat and yellow, came up over the quiet water. At last he stood and brought Megan up beside him.

"There has never been a night like this," he said when he put his arm around her. "It's a perfect night and this is the perfect place to be, here with you."

Megan rested her head against his shoulder, and they looked out over the water, content for this little space of time to let their passion wait.

"Do you know how much I've wanted you?" he asked. "Do you know how many nights I've lain below in that bed, thinking of how it would be when you were with me?" He held her away and framed her face between his hands. "Night after night I've thought of you naked in bed beside me, of your body under mine, over mine. I've thought of all the things we would do together, the ways we would love together. I've ached with wanting you, Meggie. Just as I'm aching now.''

He kissed her, and his body was hard with a need he could no longer control.

She answered his kiss, her tongue hot and silky smooth against his, and tore at the buttons of his shirt so that she could touch his fevered skin with her hands and mouth.

"Mi mujer," he whispered against the spill of her hair. *"Mi corazon."* He reached for the fastening of her white shorts, and when he tugged the shorts down over her hips, he slid his hand down inside the satin and lace strip of her panties so that he could touch her there.

"So soft and smooth," he whispered against her lips. "So warm and ready."

His fingers stroked and teased until she cried out and kissed him with all of the passion she had held in check since the moment he had come into her office that afternoon. Frantic with the need to touch him as he touched her, she unfastened his belt, and slowly, her hands trembling with eagerness, she pulled down his zipper and shoved his shorts over his hips. When she saw the hard thrust of his manhood against the thin fabric of the black bikini briefs, she whispered, "Oh, yes." And she snaked the briefs down over his hips and began to stroke him.

"Megan!" His head went back, the cords of his strong throat worked convulsively.

She had never seen a man as beautiful as he was. His coppery skin turned to bronze in the moonlight. He was magnificently naked, tall and slim, yet broad of shoulder, with sinewy muscled legs, legs that soon would bind her to him.

"Ricardo." She whispered his name in the soft night air and, still holding him there, she began to feather kisses over his face, his throat, his chest until, with a smothered cry, he scooped her up into his arms and ran across the deck to the stairs that led to the cabin below.

He had wanted to make love to her slowly tonight, to take her with tenderness, to savor every moment before that final joining. But he knew he couldn't; he had to take her quickly, with hard and primitive need.

He put her onto the bunk and pulled her panties down. Then he was over her, holding her as she held him, whispering her name in a frenzy of desire.

"I can't wait," he murmured. "I want it, but I can't."

"I don't want you to wait." She lifted her body to his and cried aloud when he grasped her hips and plunged hard into her.

He had never known such pleasure as when she opened herself to welcome him into her velvety softness. Her long, lovely legs came up around his back to hold him there. He ripped at the buttons of her shirt, heard them scatter and fall, heard the shirt tear. But it didn't matter. Nothing mattered except this moment here, now, with Meggie.

She lifted her breasts for him to suckle and moaned aloud when he took one rigid peak between his teeth to lap and tease. She kissed his shoulder, licked the skin there, and all the while she moved against him, with him, her body hot with passion and need.

"Come over me," he panted and, gripping her hips, he rolled so that she was astride him. "I want to look at you. I want to see your face and know it's as good for you as it is for me."

"It is!" she cried. "It is!"

"Ride with me, Meggie. Ride with me all the way." He reached for her breasts again, and when he did, her body began to move in frantic abandon against his. She was all woman now, rejoicing in her passion, holding nothing back, for this was her man, her lover, her husband. The years apart didn't matter; nothing mattered except that she was with him, loving him as he was loving her.

He grasped her hips. Her cadence quickened. Her skin was flushed, incandescent with a film of dewy sweat.

"Now," he gasped. "Look at me, Meggie. Look at me now!"

Everything spun out of focus. She was lost, spellbound, drowning in the depths of his amber eyes, a part of him. She was him and he was her. They were joined by flesh, by heart, by love, by their very souls. He had touched her, and she would never be the same again.

He held her close. He kissed her lips and took her cry, as she took his. Weeping with reaction, she clung to him, helpless as wave after wave of ecstasy shuddered through her body.

"Don't cry, my love," he whispered. "Don't cry, my Meggie." He took handfuls of her pale hair and held it against his face to breathe in her essence. He kissed her tender lips. He told her how good she was, how wonderful, how dear, how much she meant to him. He said all of the things she wanted to hear.

But he didn't say, "I love you."

They swam side by side, naked in the cool sea. Her hair was spread like a golden fan on the moon-kissed

waves, floating behind her when they put their arms
around each other and sank slowly beneath the surface.

Ricardo opened his eyes and looked at her. He
bound her to him with his legs. He threaded his fingers through her sea-drenched hair and kissed her
there beneath the water.

I want to live with her, he thought. I want to die
with her. I don't ever want to be separated from her
again.

They broke to the surface, gasping for air, and he
kissed her again, kissed her until they were both
breathless. And when he let her go, he took her hand
and together they swam back to the boat. He boosted
her up, one hand against her bare behind, then hoisted
himself up onto the deck. Before she could speak he
put his arms around her and drew her down onto one
of the mats. He covered her sea-slick body with his
and began to kiss her cool, salty lips. "You taste so
good," he murmured. "So good, my Meggie."

He rained kisses over her face and down her throat.
He licked her salty breasts and rubbed his face against
them before he took one tender peak to bite and kiss
gently.

And when she moaned and said, "Oh, darling, oh,
please," he began to lick his way down her salt-slick
body, kissing, taking small love bites until he reached
her warm, salty thighs, thighs that parted at his touch.

"Yes," he said against her skin. "That's it, *mi
amor, mi mujer preciosa.*"

"Ricardo," she whispered. "Oh, Ricardo."

"I have to taste you, Meggie. Have to love you like
this." He touched her with his lips. "Like this."

She cried out, and at first she tried to move away from the impossibly wonderful thing he was doing to her. But he held her there, held her while her body writhed, while she whimpered and pleaded, held her until at last she gave herself up to the sweet torture of his mouth.

She was his; he could do and would do whatever he chose to do to her because she belonged to him, as he belonged to her. No matter what happened they were lovers, man and wife, bound together by this sweet, wild, consuming love they shared.

She tightened her hands on his shoulders and lifted herself to him, and when she did, she began to spin out of control, to soar to the stars, to shatter and break, to cry out in a frenzy of passion that went on and on.

Then he was over her, his body joined to hers. "Again!" he cried. "Again for me."

Time and space converged on this one moment. They were man and woman, as elemental as the sky above them, as the sea that rocked the boat, one with the universe as they moved into a vortex of passion. He plunged and withdrew to plunge again and again.

Almost fainting with pleasure, Megan opened her eyes. His body was bathed by the moonlight. He was the ultimate male, powerful and proud in his masculinity, glorying in the pleasure he gave to his woman, bringing them closer and closer to that final explosive moment.

And when it came, for her and for him, he cried aloud, a wild and primitive cry that came from the very depths of his being.

He collapsed over her, his heart racketing hard in his chest. And Megan held him close, held him and soothed him, as he had held and soothed her.

"My love," she whispered. And at last he slept, there in the shelter of her arms.

But it was a long time before Megan slept that night. She knew now how much she loved Ricardo, and she wept, silently so that she wouldn't awaken him, for all the long and lonely years they had been apart.

And because, if he didn't love as she loved, she would have to let him go.

Chapter 12

The next morning when the wind was up they raised the sails and headed toward Plantation Key. They stood together at the wheel, bare feet braced against the roll of the boat. There was a hard chop to the water, but the sky was clear and the sun warm.

Megan loved the feel of the wind in her hair and the sharp, salty smell of the sea. And she loved the *Sea Chum*. She'd had to sacrifice other things to buy the boat, but she had never regretted it.

Three years ago a man and his wife had sailed the *Sea Chum* from Long Island. His wife had been seasick most of the way, and by the time they'd sailed down into the Keys and docked at the Gaviota, they'd barely been speaking to each other.

"Sell the damn boat," the wife had said.

He'd named Megan a price and had taken the two months he and his wife stayed at the motel as a down payment. She'd paid the rest of it off in a year and a half and had never regretted buying it. Especially now, on this fine, crisp day, standing here next to Ricardo. She put her arms around his waist, her face against his back. I love you, she thought fiercely. Whatever happens now, I'll never be sorry that I've loved you.

He brought her hand to his lips and kissed it. "I wish we had an automatic pilot. If we did, I'd set it and take you down to the cabin."

"We'd bounce all over the water in waves like this."

"That might be fun," he said. "How soon will we get to the restaurant?"

"In another hour or so."

But because of the chop, two hours went by before they got to Plantation Key and the restaurant on the water with a dock where they could tie up the *Sea Chum.* When Megan went below to change, Ricardo secured the boat.

When she came up from the cabin wearing a summer dress the same shade of blue as her eyes, he looked at her, thoughtful, unsmiling.

He wiped his hands on the sides of his jeans. "Come here." And when she did, he looked at her for one long moment without saying anything. Then he kissed her hard and deep and fast. "Wait for me," he said when he let her go.

"Ricardo..." She looked uncertain, puzzled.

He shook his head. "I won't be long."

He needed time to think, but he couldn't think when he was with her, when he was touching her or she was touching him. This rekindling of all they had once meant to each other, this incredible resurgence of passion, had caught him off guard. He knew now that he had never stopped loving her, but he also knew

what loving her and losing her had cost him emotionally.

He wanted her back, but the reason she had left him
five years ago hadn't changed. He was still the man he
had been then—stubborn, proud, a matador of brave
bulls.

She made him believe that anything was possible,
that the love they had shared hadn't died, that they
still had a chance for a life together. But did they?

When he came back out to the dock, he took her
hand and together they walked to the restaurant. As
soon as they were seated at a table overlooking the
water, he said, "We need to talk."

She glanced around the crowded room. "Shouldn't
it wait until we're back on the boat?"

"No."

The waiter brought their menus. Without looking at
his Ricardo asked, "Do you mind if I order for us?"
And when she said she didn't, he told the waiter to
bring them broiled pompano, a green salad and a
bottle of white wine.

The waiter left. Ricardo drummed his fingers on the
table and gazed out the window.

Megan's stomach tightened. This is going to be bad,
she thought. He's going to tell me that he's leaving,
that what happened between us was a mistake. His
face was serious, his expression grim. She wanted to
touch him, but she didn't.

"For the past five years," he said at last, "I've told
myself I was no longer in love with you, that I felt only
bitterness, and yes, even that I hated you for not understanding my profession and what it meant to me,
for not being woman enough to stay with me in spite

of what I did. But most of all I hated you for leaving me and for taking our child.''

''Ricardo, I—''

''I went out with other women,'' he said without giving her a chance to continue. ''I made love with other women.'' She flinched, but he didn't stop. ''I tried to find you in every woman I made love to, but when I found no comfort in being with them, I stopped trying to find another you. When I saw you again at the hospital in Mexico City, I knew nothing had changed. It wasn't just because I was grateful to you for coming, although God knows I was. I knew when I saw you that I had been lying to myself for the past five years, that I had never stopped loving you.''

He wanted to reach across the table and take her hand, but he didn't. ''I told myself I came to Florida only because of Pilar,'' he went on. ''But I came because of you, too, because I thought if I could be with you again, I could rid myself of the you who has haunted me all these years. I wanted to get you out of my heart, out of my blood, Megan. I wanted to be able to get on with my life.''

She looked stricken, afraid. He took her hand. ''But that's not what happened. We touched again, we made love again, and I knew I had never stopped loving you.'' She bowed her head to hide the tears that rose and fell, and he said, ''You've said that you love me. Do you?''

''Of course I do,'' she whispered. ''I always have. That never changed.''

''Is that why you didn't try to divorce me here in Florida?''

She nodded. ''I tried to. Three years ago. I went to see a lawyer, but I . . . I couldn't go through with it. I told myself it was because of Pilar. But it wasn't, Ricardo. It was because of us, because of what we had meant to each other. Divorce would have meant an end, and I couldn't end it. I just couldn't."

"Nor could I. And it wasn't because of the religion, Meggie. It was because I couldn't bring myself to break the only tie that bound us together."

The waiter brought their wine. Ricardo poured some into Megan's glass, then into his own before he said, "I haven't changed. I'm still the man I was eight years ago when you married me. I wouldn't give up my profession for you then and I won't give it up for you now. But I'm asking you, for both our sakes, and for Pilar, to give us another chance. I love you, but if you ever walk away from me again..." He shook his head. "I couldn't stand it if you did. It would finish everything."

She looked into his eyes and saw pride there, and the determination to be the man he was meant to be. She saw his apprehension, too, and his love, and she covered the hand that held hers and said, "I won't walk away from you, Ricardo. Not ever again."

He let out the breath he didn't even know he'd been holding. "You and Pilar..." He had to stop, to give himself a moment to get all that he was feeling under control. "You and Pilar will come back to Mexico with me when her school is out."

Megan tightened her hands around his. "Yes."

"I think it'll be all right with her. I think she'll like it that we're back together."

"Yes, she'll like it."

He raised his glass. "To a new beginning."

Megan touched her glass to his. "To a new beginning," she repeated.

"I have ten acres of land on a hill overlooking the mountains and the lake beyond," Ricardo told her that night when they lay together in the bunk. "We'll start building as soon as we return, but until our house is finished we'll live at the ranch."

He raised himself onto his elbow and looked down at her. "I know you were unhappy there before, and that you and my father don't get along, but I have to train for the coming season of corridas. I can do that at the ranch. It's better that we live there until our house is finished."

At the ranch with his father who despised her.

"How long will it take to build our house?" she asked.

"Six months. Perhaps seven."

Seven months! she wanted to say. "No, I can't do that. I *won't* do that again." But she would do as he asked because she loved him, and because that love was still fragile.

"There's something else we should talk about." He laid his hand on her stomach. "I don't know how you feel about it, but we need to discuss whether or not we want to have another child. You're not on the Pill, are you?"

She shook her head. "There's been no reason to be." She sat up, her eyes wide with apprehension. "I...we...we haven't taken any precautions. This all happened so fast that I didn't think..." She stared at him. "I might already be pregnant!"

"Would you mind very much if you were?"

"No. I don't know." She fell back against the pillows. Pregnant? A new baby? Morning sickness? A brother or a sister for Pilar. A little boy who looked like Ricardo. She shook her head. "I don't know," she said again.

"If you don't want to—"

"I didn't say that. It's just that I never thought I'd ever have another baby."

"We'll see a doctor Monday if you want to start on the Pill."

"Maybe it's already too late."

He kissed her, and moving his hand down her belly, he said, "If it's already too late, I don't suppose another few times will make much difference."

She closed her eyes as his hand slipped down to the apex of her legs. "No," she whispered. "I don't suppose it will."

"Well, then . . ."

It will be all right, she thought when he joined his body to hers. If they had already made a baby, she would love it just as much as she loved Pilar. As much as she loved Ricardo.

As she lifted her body to welcome him, Megan smiled. Tonight might very well be the night.

Robert Benson, Willie Bob's father, brought Pilar back to the motel at five o'clock on Sunday afternoon. Megan was in the kitchen making lasagne while Ricardo made the salad.

"*Hola, muchacha,*" he said when Pilar ran to hug him, and when she went to kiss Megan, he shook hands with Benson and ruffled Willie Bob's red hair.

"Thank you for bringing Pilar back safely," he told the man. "I didn't know you were still home on leave."

"I go back day after tomorrow," Benson said. "My time is almost up, so I'll be stateside for my last two months." He ran his hand through hair that was almost the same bright red as his son's. "I'll be going back to school to finish my degree just as soon as I get some kind of a job and find a different place for the three of us to live."

"Well, good luck, and thank you, and your wife, too, for looking after Pilar this weekend."

"You were nice to my boy when he was in the hospital, Mr. Montoya. We're both of us mighty grateful." He put his hand on Willie Bob's shoulder. "We've got to be running along now. My missus is waiting for us out in the car."

"Please thank her for me," Megan said.

"I will, ma'am. But your little girl wasn't any trouble at all. Anyway, she and old Willie Bob are friends. He'd have been mighty unhappy if she hadn't come along."

"Would not!" Willie Bob crossed his eyes and stuck out his tongue.

"Yech," Pilar said when father and son were out of sight. "He's horrible!"

Megan smiled at Ricardo over her daughter's head, and he smiled back. "Can dinner wait for a little while?" he asked.

And when Megan said that it could, he took Pilar's hand. "Let's the three of us go into the other room," he said. "Your mother and I have something to tell you."

Pilar looked at one, then the other. "Is it something bad?" she asked, her small face serious.

"No," Megan said. "It's something good." She motioned Pilar to the sofa and sat down beside her. Ricardo sat on the chair facing them.

"Your father and I . . ." Megan took a deep breath. "Your father and I are going to live together again, Pilar."

Pilar's eyes widened. "Really? Do you mean it? You're really and truly going to get unseparated?"

"Really and truly," Megan said.

"And we're going to be a family again?"

"Yes, Pilar." Ricardo held his arms out, and when she went to him, he pulled her up on his lap. "I hope that makes you happy."

"It does!" She hugged him, then she looked at Megan. "Where are we going to live, Mom?"

"In Mexico, honey. As soon as your school's out, the three of us will go back there together. Your dad's going to build us a brand-new house to live in, but until it's done we'll stay on your grandfather's ranch."

"Neat! I really liked it there. Will I have my own room, or will I have to sleep with you?"

"You'll have your own room," Ricardo said. "And your mother and I will have our own room."

"Together?" Pilar looked at him, then at her mother, and frowned.

"In the meantime," Megan said, aware of Pilar's look of disapproval, "your dad's going to move in here with us. You see, Pilar, when moms and dads get . . ." She hesitated, then, using Pilar's words, said, "When they get unseparated, they sleep in the same bedroom."

"Oh." Pilar looked thoughtful, then she nodded and asked, "And Dad's going to be living with us from now on?"

"From now on," Megan said.

"I hope that's all right with you." Ricardo kissed her cheek. "I love you and your mother very much,

Pilar, and I want to be with both of you from now on.''

''Forever and ever?''

''Forever and ever.''

She slid off his lap. ''Is it okay if I go and call Willie Bob and tell him we're going to Mexico?''

''Why don't you wait until after dinner?'' Ricardo suggested. ''I'm going to call his father later, so you can talk to him then.'' He looked at Megan. ''I don't know whether or not you want to sell the Gaviota, but if you don't, we could hire someone to manage it. That way we could come back once in a while, maybe several times a year.''

''You're thinking of the Bensons, aren't you?''

Ricardo nodded. ''I like Robert Benson. Would you mind if I talked to him about it?''

Megan was thoughtful for a moment. ''No. Call him. I think I'd like to keep the Gaviota, at least for a while, and with the Bensons here, and Agnes and Tyrone, I'd know it would be in good hands.''

''Willie Bob would be living here?'' Pilar made a face, then grinned and said, ''That's all right, I guess. I mean, he's awful and everything, but I'm kinda used to him.''

She talked nonstop all through dinner—about the shark she'd seen from the glass-bottomed boat, the stingrays in the aquarium and about all of the things that went on at the wharf at sunset. ''There were fire-eaters. And magicians and clowns and music, and then the sun went down and everybody went home.''

''It's going to be all right,'' Ricardo said when Pilar excused herself from the table. ''My moving into your room, I mean.''

"Our room." Megan reached across the table and took his hand.

Later, when they kissed their daughter good-night, they went into their room and he closed the door.

"My wife," he said. And took her into his arms.

When the big silver jet soared into a cloudless sky, Megan looked down on the city of Miami and on the narrow strip of oceanfront that was Miami Beach. For a moment, but only for a moment, she felt a twinge of sadness because she was leaving Florida and the life she had known there for the past five years. This was a big step, a final step, for though they would return to Florida from time to time, their home would be in Mexico.

She thought of the months ahead, and of the years. Ricardo had told her that in time, perhaps in another ten years, he would give up bullfighting. "I'll raise bulls for other men to fight then," he'd said. "And we'll travel. But until then I'll continue to fight."

"But your legs," she'd said. "I've seen you limping, Ricardo. I'm worried about your legs."

"It's only when I'm tired," he had protested. "It's nothing. I need more exercise, that's all."

"You've been swimming every day and you run every morning."

"I'm stronger every day. I have almost all of my old strength back. The limp is nothing."

But she knew that it was, and she was afraid.

Isabel met their plane when they landed in Mexico City. She hugged Pilar, then threw her arms around Megan.

"I'm so happy!" she cried. "I couldn't believe it when you and Ricardo phoned to tell us the two of you had decided to get back together. It's wonderful news. Wonderful!" She stood on tiptoe and kissed Ricardo. "*Felicidades, hermanito.* I couldn't be happier." Then she looped her arm through Pilar's and said, "Fernando is taking all of us out for a celebration dinner tonight. We're going to a lovely restaurant in Chapultepec Park. There's a lagoon and swans—"

"I had planned on going right out to the ranch," Ricardo said.

"You can go tomorrow."

"But I told father I'd come directly out from the plane."

"And *I* told him you were spending the night in the city, so no arguments, brother mine. Tonight we're celebrating that at last you've had the good sense to bring Megan and Pilar back here where they belong."

He smiled and put his arm around Megan. "And this is where she'll stay."

Pilar, happy to see her parents together again and excited about being back in Mexico offered no objection when Ricardo asked if she minded staying with the maid while they went out.

"It's kind of an adult night," he said. "Lupita will fix something special for you and you can watch TV, all right?"

"Okay," she said and kissed his cheek.

Dinner that night was a festive occasion, a celebration for Megan and Ricardo to mark the joy of their being back together again.

Fernando ordered French champagne, and when it was served, he raised his glass and said, "To Ricardo and Megan. *Amor, salud y pesetas. Y tiempo para gastarlas.* Love, health and money. And time to enjoy them." He clinked his glass to each of theirs. "Isabel and I wish both of you a lifetime of happiness. And to you, Ricardo, brave bulls for you to fight for many years to come."

Ricardo smiled and raised his glass. And didn't see the look that Megan and Isabel exchanged, or the sudden fear in Megan's eyes.

When the orchestra began to play, Ricardo took her hand and led her out onto the dance floor. She had worn an elegantly simple white silk dress that made her look ladylike yet sexy. "You look beautiful tonight. Are you happy to be back?"

"Yes, I'm happy." She looked around her—at the dancing couples, at the crystal chandeliers and at the flickering candles on the pristine white tablecloths. "I love Mexico City. In spite of the crowds and the smog and the traffic, I love being here."

"But it will be good to get back to the ranch tomorrow." He tightened his arms around her. "That's where we belong, Meggie, not here in the city."

She leaned her head against his shoulder. That's where you belong, my love, she thought. But is it where I belong? She loved Ricardo, and with all her heart she had committed herself to him. Yet she couldn't rid herself of a small shadow of doubt, not of her love or his, but of what it would be like when they were once again living at the ranch with his parents. And of how she would feel when he began to train, when the time came for him to face the bulls again.

A shiver ran through her body. He felt it and asked, "What is it, Meggie? Are you cold?"

"It's nothing," she said. "Just an old ghost walking over my grave."

They went back to the table. They drank more champagne. Ricardo and Fernando talked about the bulls. "How soon will you be able to fight again?" Fernando asked.

"In another month," Ricardo said. "I've talked to Dad. He's arranged corridas for me in Mexico City and Guadalajara."

Megan was silent. She looked at him over her glass of champagne, but she said nothing because there was nothing to say. He had told her he wouldn't change, that he would continue to fight, and she had accepted him on those terms. But, oh, how she wanted to cling to him, to keep him safe. She wanted to say, "No, don't fight again. I don't want you to fight again." But she couldn't. And she thought, What if I lost him? Oh, my God! What if I lost him? I couldn't survive. I wouldn't want to.

When they danced again, she held him as tightly as she could. And she said, "Make love to me tonight, Ricardo."

"I plan to." He smiled, then his face sobered and he asked, "Is anything wrong, Meggie?"

"No, it's just that I..." She shook her head, made herself smile and said, "It's the champagne. It makes me feel..." She tried to smile. "Ready."

He chuckled and drew her closer into his arms. "If it makes you feel like that, I'll buy a case in the morning."

When they went back to the table, he said, "It's getting late. I think we'd better call it a night."

On the way back to Isabel and Fernando's he could feel the tension in Megan. In the darkness of the back seat her hand was warm against his thigh, and when the car swerved, she leaned against him, closer than the swerve warranted so that her breast brushed against him.

"Would you like some coffee?" Isabel asked when they reached the house.

"No," Ricardo said. "It's late. Really. Thank you for a wonderful evening." He took Megan's hand. "We'll see you in the morning."

They went to the guest room, and when he closed the door, he pulled her close and kissed her.

"Love me tonight," she said against his lips. "Love me like you'll never let me go."

She stepped away and pulled the white dress up over her head. She was wearing a white lace teddy and sheer stockings.

He looked at her, and with a muffled cry he picked her up and carried her to the bed.

She gripped his shoulders and brought him down over her. She tasted his mouth and dueled a silken duel with his tongue. She fumbled with his belt. "Hurry," she whispered. "Hurry."

"Meggie? *Por Dios,* Meggie!" He yanked his belt open, then tore at his trousers, as excited as she was now, unable to wait, wanting her the way she wanted him.

She reached for him, and with a cry he gripped her hips and joined his body to hers.

"Yes," she gasped. "Oh, yes, like that." She coiled her arms and legs around his back to hold him there, to press him closer because this way, for this time that they were alone, he belonged to her. She could keep him safe.

She lifted her body to his and sought his mouth. She kissed his throat, his shoulders, his chest. "More," she whispered. "Give me more."

He was on fire, blazing with a crazy kind of passion. This was a different Meggie, a pagan queen offering herself up to the god of love. But he wasn't a god; he was only a man, a man who loved her.

Loved her. His body thundered against hers, and she clung to him, whispering, "Yes, oh, yes, like that."

Then he could no longer wait and he said, "Now, Meggie. Now!" And when she cried out and he felt her body rise to his, his body exploded in a paroxysm of feeling unlike anything he had ever known.

When it ended and he could get his breath, he tightened his arms around her. Small shudders shivered through her, muted sighs escaped her lips. She kissed his mouth. "I love you," she said.

The next day they left for the ranch.

Chapter 13

"I'm so filled with joy that you've come back to us." Josefa, who had been waiting in the patio for their arrival, embraced Pilar and Megan. Then, taking Ricardo's hand, she brought him closer to Megan and placed his hand in hers. Holding their two hands bound to hers, she said, "This is the way you should be, together, for always."

Ricardo's gaze met Megan's. "For always." He kissed his mother's cheek. *"Gracias, Mamá."*

And Megan, her heart overflowing with gladness and with the certainty that she had made the right decision, repeated, "For always."

When Josefa let them go, she led the way into the house. "Franco is out at the stable," she said. "One of the mares is about to foal."

"Which one?" Ricardo asked.

"Sultana. You remember her, don't you, Ricardo? She had a difficult time before and Franco is con-

cerned. If you'd like to go out to the stables, I know
your father would be glad for your help. Meantime,
I'll show Megan and Pilar their rooms. We'll have
dinner tonight at eight."

"*Muy bien, Madre.* And let's make dinner tonight
a special occasion, shall we?" He smiled a decep-
tively innocent smile at Megan. "It would be nice if we
had champagne."

She felt hot color rush to her cheeks because she was
embarrassed by the way she had behaved last night.
But now Ricardo was looking at her as though he
hadn't at all minded, and spurred on by that look she
smiled back at him and said, "Yes, champagne would
be nice."

He gave her an I'll-see-you-later look, and to his
mother he said, "I'll go on out to the stable with Dad
then."

Pilar took hold of his hand. "Can I go with you?"

"I don't think so, Pilar. A lady horse is giving birth,
and I'm not sure you—"

"She's having a baby? A baby horse?" Pilar clasped
her hands together. "I want to see! Can I, Dad?
Please?"

He looked at Megan. "What do you think?"

"I think it would be all right," she said. "If your
father won't mind."

Ricardo hesitated. "It will be all right, but I'm
afraid it might be a little too strange and scary for you
Pilar. The mare will be in a lot of pain and she'll try to
thrash around."

"I'll be careful, Dad."

"You'll have to stay well out of the way. If you're
afraid or bothered by what you see and you want to
leave, just tell me."

Her chin, a miniature of his, firmed. "I won't be afraid."

"All right, if you're sure you want to." He embraced his mother, gave Megan a quick kiss and took Pilar's hand.

"You cannot imagine the joy it gives me to see him with her," Josefa said when father and daughter disappeared through the stand of pepper trees that shielded the stables from the house. "Ricardo isn't a man who displays his emotions for everyone to see, but these last years have been difficult for him, as I'm sure they have for you. It's good to see the three of you reunited as a family again."

She motioned to two of the servants to pick up their luggage as she and Megan started down the long, open corridor with the old stone arches that led to the bedrooms. At the far end of the corridor Josefa opened one of the doors and motioned Megan inside.

"When Ricardo telephoned to tell me that you and Pilar were returning with him, I added a few things to your room that I thought might make you more comfortable. When you and Pilar were here at Christmas, you were in one of the guest rooms, but this is your room, yours and Ricardo's. I hope it pleases you."

It was a lovely, spacious room. The walls were blush ivory. The thick pile carpet and the drapes were ivory-gold, as was the quilted satin spread that covered the four-poster canopied bed. There was a stone fireplace against one wall, an old-fashioned armoire and double dressers against another. A small round table, graced with a bouquet of pink roses, and two cushioned ladder-back chairs had been placed in front of the shadow-curtained French doors that led out into a small private garden.

It was one of the most beautiful rooms Megan had ever seen. She put her arms around Ricardo's mother and said, *"Gracias. Muchas gracias, Doña Josefa."*

"I wanted everything to be nice for you and Ricardo." Josefa's fine, dark eyes, so like Ricardo's, were kind. "He never stopped loving you, Megan. In his heart you've always been his wife. That has never changed. And you're my daughter, just as Isabel is. I'm glad you've come home again."

"Oh, so am I," Megan said. "So am I."

"Remember," Ricardo said, "if any of this bothers you, I want you to tell me and we'll leave."

Pilar shook her head. "I'm not a sissy, Dad. Besides, I know all about how baby animals are born."

"You do?" He tried to keep the surprise out of his voice.

"Willie Bob told me. He was home alone when his dog had puppies, and he saw them come out. I suppose it's the same with horses except that they're bigger."

"A lot bigger," he said, and led her into the stable.

His father and one of the ranch workers were on their knees beside the mare. There was fresh straw in the stall, and sunlight from a high window. The mare's belly was distended. She was in distress, rolling her eyes, trying to get up.

"Hola, Ricardo." Franco turned away from the mare. "I thought you were coming yesterday." He looked at Pilar and frowned. "What is the girl doing here?"

"I want to see the mother horse have her baby." Pilar stepped closer to Ricardo.

"This is no place for children," he said in English.

"I'm seven years old."

"You're a child and you're a female."

"So's the lady horse."

His frown became ferocious. "She shouldn't be here," Franco told Ricardo in Spanish.

"Pilar won't be in the way, Father." Ricardo patted Pilar's shoulder. "Wait here," he said, and went into the stall. He knelt down beside the mare and rubbed her flanks. "How is she?" he asked his father.

"She's coming along. It won't be long now."

A shudder went through the mare. She whinnied and tried to stand.

"Easy, girl," Ricardo murmured. "Easy, Sultana."

"It has started again, *señor*," the helper said.

Pilar climbed up on the second rung of the stall gate and looped her arms over the top rung so that she could see into the stall. She wanted to ask her father to do something to help the animal but knew that she shouldn't bother either him or her grim-faced grandfather. The horse snorted in pain. Pilar swallowed hard, but she didn't move away.

"I've got to help her," Franco muttered. "It's been going on too long. Ricardo, you and José will have to hold her." He rolled up his shirtsleeves. "Steady, girl. Steady," he said as he reached up inside the mare.

She whinnied in pain and tried to move away, but Ricardo and José held her. Franco was on his hands and knees, his head against the mare's flank, almost all of his arm inside her. He was sweating, panting with effort. "*Sí, sí,* I have it, it's coming now. Hold the mare steady."

Two legs and the lower half of the foal's body were visible. "A little more." Franco's face was strained.

He grunted, "Come on. Come on now..." And the foal, covered with the thin, glistening, transparent veil of afterbirth, was born.

It wobbled, and still attached to its mother by that thin, silvery membrane, tried to stand.

"Oh!" And though the word was barely a whisper, the three men turned and looked up at Pilar. Her hands were clasped together, great fat tears rolled down her cheeks.

"I told you you shouldn't have brought her in here," Franco said angrily. "The child's upset. She—"

"She's not upset." Ricardo smiled gently at his daughter. "Are you, Pilar?"

So overcome by emotion she could barely speak, in a voice that trembled, she said, "Daddy, that's... that's the most beautiful thing I've ever seen." She let herself down from the rungs. "Can I see the baby? Can I touch him?"

"Let me wipe him off first, *querida*."

Pilar took a step forward and very tentatively put her hand on her grandfather's shoulder. "You helped the mother have her baby," she said softly. Her small face was solemn, and her eyes looked almost too big for her face. "I think what you did was the most wonderful thing I ever saw in my whole life."

Franco cleared his throat. "The mare's a prize animal. It would cost me money to lose her." He got to his feet and brushed the straw off the knees of his trousers. "Well, go ahead. Pet the foal if you want to."

She stroked the silky nose. "He's so soft," she whispered. "And he's beautiful, isn't he, Dad?"

"Beautiful." Ricardo rested his hand on Pilar's head. "Beautiful," he said again.

"Look at his legs. They're so skinny, and those white marks make him look like he's wearing stockings."

"You and the girl go on back to the house, Ricardo."Franco wiped his hands off with a clean towel. "José and I will finish up. Then I have to see to the other horses."

Pilar rubbed the foal's neck. "Can I stay here with the baby, Grandfather?"

He shook his head. "Go on back to the house with your father. I've got work to do here."

"I could help."

Franco, legs apart, hands on his hips, glowered down at her.

She glowered back at him, her jaw thrust out, sixty pounds of determination.

"You don't know anything about horses," he said.

"You could teach me."

"You'll only be in the way."

"No, I won't." Her mouth softened into a smile. "Please?"

Franco ran a hand down the side of his jaw. He looked at Ricardo, then back at Pilar. "All right, you can stay. But you obey orders. Is that clear?"

"Yep."

"Do you want to name the colt?"

Her eyes widened. She looked from her grandfather to her father and back to the colt. "Yes. Oh, yes!"

"*Muy bien.* What is it going to be?"

She closed her eyes and took a deep breath. "Prince. No, no, wait . . . White Stocking Prince, because he looks like he's wearing white stockings."

"¡Dios mío!" Franco frowned again. "Are you sure?"

"Absolutely." Pilar grinned up at him. "White Stocking Prince."

Franco sighed, then nodded reluctantly. "Very well. From now on he's your horse and you've got to take care of him. He—"

"He's my horse." She looked at her father, not sure she'd heard right. "Mine?"

"That's what I said." Franco motioned to the stall next to the one they were in. "It needs cleaning. Let's see what kind of a job you can do."

"Yes, *sir.*" She grinned at her father. "I'll see you later. I've got to go to work now."

He squeezed her shoulder. *"Gracias,"* he said to his father. *"Mil gracias, Papá."*

"Ya, ya. I'll take Pilar back to the house in a little while. She'll be all right. Don't worry about her."

"I won't," Ricardo said.

And when he got back to the house, to the room he and Megan would share, he said, "You should have seen Pilar, Meggie. She stood up to Father. He was tough, but she stuck out her chin and stood her ground." He laughed. "I think my father has finally met his match. He's crazy about her."

Megan smiled, glad for Pilar's sake that Franco had accepted her. She didn't mind Franco's not liking her—she could put up with that and not say anything—but she knew that if he had taken his animosity for her out on Pilar, she wouldn't have stood still for it. And because he had accepted Pilar, perhaps in time he might even come to accept her.

Perhaps.

Ricardo was up every morning at five-thirty. He ran for an hour through pasture lands, up mountain trails with rough terrain, then down and around the pond where the ranch animals came to drink. Toward the end of the run he was panting with strain and doing his damnedest to ignore the pain in his legs. When his legs began to tremble and he knew that if he didn't stop he would fall, he slowed to a walk. And cursed his legs and the goring that had weakened them.

He was determined to get his strength back, to do whatever he had to do, to run in spite of the pain and the weakness, to go on until he dropped. And sometimes he did. And when he fell, he would lie there alone where no one could see him and curse his legs. Then he would pick himself up and run on. Nothing would stop him, he vowed. Nothing.

He had three fights scheduled before the Estoque de Oro—two in Mexico City and one in Guadalajara. He would be ready for them, and yes, by God, he would be ready to participate in the Estoque de Oro.

By six-thirty every morning he was back at the house so that he could shower and have a light breakfast with Megan and Pilar. Afterward he would walk across the fields to the bullring where Juan Larrea waited.

Juan, a retired matador and a contemporary of Franco's, had volunteered to help Ricardo train. A short bandy-legged man with a suntanned face, a thatch of pure white hair and a walrus moustache, Juan was a hard taskmaster.

"The legs," he said to Ricardo that first morning. "We must strengthen the legs if you want to place your own banderillas."

Ricardo always had, but he knew it took agility and strong legs to place the colorful wooden sticks with the steel-barbed point at one end. To place them the matador had to cut in on and across the bull's charge, timing his run so that when he and the bull came together he would be one step ahead of the animal. When the bull lowered his head to hook, the man had to bring his feet together, raise the banderillas and, as he passed the horns, plunge in the sticks. This was the dangerous moment, the moment when the bull raised his head to gore, the moment when the matador had to pivot quickly away.

It took great courage for a man to do this. He had the courage; it was the strength in his legs that worried him.

He practiced running backward and sideways. He worked endless hours with a helper who held the *pitones de mano,* a hand-held set of horns. He worked with the cape and the muleta until his arms ached. He did everything Larrea told him to do, and more.

Each late afternoon he returned to the house to shower and change before dinner. He would try to hide his fatigue when he came out of the bathroom with the towel wrapped around his waist, and it angered him when Megan would say, "You've done too much today, Ricardo. You've worn yourself out. You're tired."

"I'm fine," he'd snap. "I'm as good now as I was before the accident."

"I wish you'd take it easier."

"I don't want to take it easier. I'm going to fight in Mexico City in three weeks. I have to be ready."

And when her face tightened and her lips compressed, he would turn away so that he wouldn't have to see the fear in her eyes.

But there were other times when her face would soften and she would say, "Come lie down, Ricardo. Let me rub your back." And she would lock the door of their room, and he would lay naked face down on the bed and let her minister to him.

She would begin with his shoulders and his neck, rubbing hard, bearing down, kneading with her fingers. The warmth of her hands would seep into his bones, and at last he would relax and give himself up to the hands that soothed and took the pain away.

When she finished with his back, she would straddle him so that she could massage his legs. Slowly she would work her way up from his feet to the calves, and he would say, "*Sí,* like that. Yes, that's good." And when she massaged his thighs and buttocks, his body would tighten because it was good and because he knew that when she finished they would make love.

"I love to touch you like this," she'd say. "I love the feel of your skin." And when he made as though to turn, she would whisper, "Not yet, Ricardo. Not yet." And she would run her hands beneath his hips, touch him and say, "This is part of the massage, Ricardo. I have to touch you everywhere, darling."

And though his body was taut with wanting her, she would make him wait until at last, when he could no longer bear it, he would roll her beneath him, rip the bikini panties down and enter her.

Those were the good times. When he was with her like that, he could almost forget the coming corridas, and the weakness in his legs.

There wasn't enough for Megan to do. She tried to help Josefa with the running of the house, but there were servants to do most of the work. Besides, Josefa had been running her household for almost forty years and she didn't need any help.

That was difficult for Megan. For the past five years she had been in charge of a successful business. She missed the work, the guests who had come year after year. She missed Agnes and Tyrone.

The Bensons had moved into the largest efficiency. They were happy there and business was good. She wasn't worried, but she missed the activity.

Pilar helped out at the stables, Ricardo was in training, but there wasn't anything for her to do. When she picked flowers from Josefa's garden, the gardener gave her dirty looks. When she tried to help out in the kitchen, the cook took it as a personal affront and went running to Josefa in tears, insisting the Señora Gringa was trying to take over her kitchen.

"I don't know what to do with myself," she told Isabel when they met in Mexico City for lunch. "I'm used to working. Now there isn't anything for me to do and I'm bored."

"But you're Ricardo's wife," Isabel said, puzzled. "Isn't that enough?"

"Yes, but..." Megan shook her head. "I love Ricardo, Isabel, and I want to be a good wife, but I can't stand just sitting around with nothing to do."

"It will be different when you have your own home. Then, even though you have servants, you'll be in charge. There will be plenty for you to do."

Megan took a bite of her fettuccine. "I suppose so." She shook her head. "I don't know what's the matter with me lately. I love Ricardo and I'm happy to be living in Mexico again. Pilar has adjusted well. She loves your mother and father and she's as happy as a bird. It's me. I'm nervous and irritable, and I don't feel all that well."

"Are you ill? What is it?"

"Nothing really. Probably just the change in the climate and the water. I've been having morning queasies. It isn't anything, really."

"Maybe you're pregnant."

"No...I don't think so."

But suddenly Megan wasn't all that sure. The weekend after she and Ricardo had talked about marriage she had gone to a doctor in Tavernier. It wasn't that she didn't want to have a baby; it was just that she wanted to give both herself and Ricardo time to get used to each other again. Ricardo understood and agreed, and she'd started on the Pill that week.

But she could have gotten pregnant before she'd started on the Pill.

Before she left the city that day she agreed to let Isabel make a doctor's appointment for her the following week.

Meantime she decided not to say anything to Ricardo.

Chapter 14

The next two mornings Megan was too ill to get up for breakfast.

"What is it?" Ricardo asked when he came in from his run. Her face was pale, damp with perspiration, and she was unsteady on her feet. "You're ill," he said, and helped her back to bed.

"Probably Montezuma out for revenge on another *gringa*." Megan tried to smile. "Maybe I ate too much chicken mole last night."

"And maybe you should see a doctor."

"I have an appointment next week," she said when she saw his concern. "I'm sure this isn't anything, Ricardo. I've been eating different food, drinking different water. And remember, I've been living at sea level for five years. San Rafael is almost seven thousand feet. That takes a little getting used to."

"We've been here for over two weeks," he said.

"Then I'm going to start feeling better any day now." She reached for his hand. "Go take your shower, darling. I'm fine, really."

Fine but probably pregnant. Megan closed her eyes and tried to coax her queasy stomach to settle down. She would go to the doctor as she had said, but she knew what he would say because she'd had all these same symptoms with Pilar, not as severe as these, but similar enough to be recognizable.

She would have to tell Ricardo, of course, but she didn't want to tell him now when he had so much on his mind. This weekend there would be a *tienta* here at the ranch, and a week after that he would fight for the first time since the goring. She would wait until she had seen the doctor, until she was absolutely sure that her suspicions were true before she told him.

She wasn't sorry that she was pregnant, but she would have preferred to wait until they were in their own home. The way that was going it might take forever. Ricardo had contacted and talked to an architect. The architect had drawn up plans, but the plans hadn't yet been approved, so the building hadn't started.

"I've been busy," Ricardo told Megan when she asked how soon construction would begin. "But I promise we'll make a date with the architect soon."

Soon wasn't soon enough. She wanted to be in her own home now.

Megan stayed in bed that day. She felt better the next morning, and a little after nine, when the rest of the house was quiet, she went into the dining room for breakfast. Too late she realized that Franco was there, alone at the head of the table, reading the *Excelsior*.

"Good morning," she said. At a sideboard she dished strawberries onto a small plate, added a warm *bolillo* and poured herself a cup of tea.

"Ricardo tells me you haven't been feeling well," Franco said when she sat down. "He said perhaps the water here in Mexico had made you ill." He snapped the newspaper closed. "Or is it our food that you don't like?"

Megan carefully set down the cup of tea. "I'm afraid Ricardo misunderstood. I said the change in water may have bothered me, as well as the difference in altitude."

For a moment Franco was silent. He finished his coffee and wiped his mouth before he looked at her down the length of the table. "I must say I was surprised when Ricardo phoned to tell us you would be returning to Mexico with him."

Megan waited.

"Why did you?"

"I beg your pardon?"

"Why did you come back?"

"Because I love him," she said quietly.

"Oh?" Franco tapped his fingers against the folded newspaper. "You professed to love him when you married him, too, yet you stayed with him for less than three years. How long do you plan to stay this time?"

Something twisted in Megan's stomach. She wanted to get up and run away, but she didn't. This confrontation had been coming since the day she'd arrived. It was time to face it, and Franco.

"You tried to change Ricardo," Franco said. "It didn't matter to you what he wanted. You wanted him to leave the life he loved, the life he still loves. You did it once and you'll do it again."

"No." Megan shook her head. "I was afraid," she said as calmly as she could. "But I've changed. I won't interfere with whatever Ricardo wants to do." She crumpled the white linen napkin into a ball. "I don't want to fight with you, Franco. You're Ricardo's father. I—"

He gripped the newspaper as he would a weapon. "Why couldn't you have left him alone?" he growled. "Why did you insist he go back to Florida with you?"

"It was for Pilar. He's her father. He—"

"It wasn't because of Pilar. It was because you decided you wanted him back. You wanted him to go to Florida with you so you could seduce him into taking you back."

"No…" Sickness rose in her throat, and she dug her nails into her palms so that she wouldn't be ill. "I love Ricardo. I never stopped loving him."

"Love? You married Ricardo because of who he was—a rising young matador—and because he came from a wealthy family. Once you had him you tried to change him, to make him to be a *gringo* husband." He slapped the rolled-up newspaper so hard against the table that Megan flinched. "What kind of love is it that tries to change a man?" he went on. "Maybe that's what women do in your country, but a Mexican woman knows better. She…"

"Please," Megan said. "Don't do this."

But he went on, unmindful of how white her face was or of the sickness he saw in her eyes. "He should have married a woman of his own kind. A Mexican woman." He took a step closer. "Go back where you came from, Megan. Leave my son alone."

Megan pushed her chair back and stood up. "No," she said, facing him. "I left him once because of you, because you told me my fear would kill him. I left because I was afraid to fight you. I—'' The floor tilted. She gripped the edge of the table. She wanted to beg him to stop, wanted to sink back into a chair and cover her face with her hands. But she didn't. She sucked in a great gulp of air and said, "Maybe in time I could have learned to live with my fear, Franco. But you didn't give me a chance. You never gave me a chance.''

"Because you weren't one of us. You had no business being here. You were a *gringa*." He took a step toward her. "I got rid of you once," he said in a low, threatening voice. "I'll get rid of you again. I—''

"That's enough!" Ricardo, his face tight with anger, strode into the room. "How dare you speak to Megan that way? How *dare* you?" He put his arm around her. "What did he mean that he got rid of you once? Tell me?"

"He said..." She took a napkin off the table and held it to her lips. "He told me...before...that my fear would kill you. I believed him. I..." She swallowed. "Maybe he was right, Ricardo. Maybe if I had stayed..." The floor tilted. She grabbed at the back of a chair, but her knees were too weak to hold her. She clutched Ricardo's arm and closed her eyes. "I don't feel well," she murmured.

"I didn't know she was ill," his father said.

Ricardo shouldered his way past him. "Get out of my way."

The color drained from Franco's face. "You don't understand, Ricardo. I only wanted what was best for you. You were on your way to being the best matador in Mexico since Arruza. Your career was the most important thing in your life. It—''

"My wife and my child were more important. I didn't know it then, but I know it now."

"Ricardo, wait . . ."

Franco put his hand on Ricardo's arm, but Ricardo brushed past him. "Get out of my way. I have to take care of my wife."

He carried her down the corridor to their room and placed her on their bed. Her eyes were closed, her face white. "I'm going to call a doctor," he said, and picked up the bedside telephone receiver.

"No, wait. I'll be all right in a minute. I'm going to see the doctor in Mexico City next week, Ricardo. I'd really rather wait until then."

"You should see somebody now."

"No, please. Let's wait."

Reluctantly he put the receiver down. Then he took her hands and asked, "Why didn't you tell me about my father, Megan? I didn't know. I had no idea he'd said those things to you. You should have told me a long time ago."

She touched the side of his face. "But you see, I thought he was right, Ricardo. And in a way he was. I did want you to quit. I hated it every time you walked into a bullring. I'd have done anything I could to have stopped you, anything to make you turn and walk away and never fight again. I was so afraid, Ricardo, but my biggest fear was what my fear would do to you. I believed your father when he told me that my fear would kill you. I believe that *he* believed it. That's why I want you to forgive him. He's your father. You mean everything to him."

"And you mean everything to me." He lay down beside her and took her into his arms, not with passion but with the need to hold her close, to comfort her and to be comforted by her. "You're my life, Meggie," he said. "You're my everything."

And when she began to be drowsy and her eyes closed, he kissed her gently and said, "Sleep with the angels, my love," and held her while she slept.

"You're two months pregnant." The doctor, a tall, spare man in his early sixties, put down the report he had been reading and looked across his desk at Megan.

She took a deep breath.

"You are pleased, *señora?*"

"Yes, I'm pleased."

"Your baby will be born somewhere around the middle of April, the nineteenth or twentieth, I believe." He consulted her file again. "You have another child. Was it an easy pregnancy?"

"Yes, it was. I became pregnant while we were in Spain. My husband had a full schedule of corridas and we traveled a lot. It didn't seem to hurt me."

"But it has been...what? Seven years since your last pregnancy?"

"Eight," Megan said.

"And you're older." He smiled at her from across his desk. "Not that much older, of course, but it's best to be careful. You'll need to get proper rest, eat well and take the vitamins I'm going to prescribe. I'd tell you to avoid too much excitement, but I suppose that's impossible now that your husband is strong enough to fight again. He's a great matador, *señora*. You must be proud of him."

"I am," Megan said. "Of course."

Of course.

Isabel was waiting for her when she came out of the doctor's office. "Well?" she asked. "What is it?"

"A severe case of..." Megan paused.

"*¡Dios mío!* Of what?"

"Of pregnancy," Megan said.

"You're pregnant?" Isabel hugged her. "That's wonderful news!"

"Yes, it is." And now that it was fact rather than conjecture it really was wonderful news.

"When are you due?" Isabel asked.

"The middle of April."

"An April child. How lovely, Megan. Have you told Ricardo?"

"Not yet. I wanted to wait until I was sure." She looked at Isabel. "Please don't say anything until I tell him."

"I won't." Isabel smiled. "Mama will be so pleased, Megan. So will my father."

"Will he?"

"Yes, of course." Isabel hesitated. "What is it? Is something wrong?"

"Your father and I had words," Megan said, and didn't add that because they had everybody in the family was upset. Ricardo barely spoke to his father. Pilar, who spent most of every day with Franco, looked anxious and upset. Dinner was a harrowing experience. Josefa tried to make conversation and Pilar tried to help. Ricardo ignored his father, and Franco said little more than, "Pass the tortillas."

It was unpleasant for all of them.

"Papa can be difficult," Isabel said when they started out to the car. "But when he hears you're pregnant again he'll be pleased." She linked Megan's arm through hers. "It's going to be all right. He can be difficult, but he has a good side, too."

Perhaps he has, Megan thought when she drove back out to the ranch that day after seeing the doctor, but he certainly had never shown it to her.

When she parked and went in, she saw Josefa in the flower-filled patio.

"We must talk," Ricardo's mother said.

And though Megan dreaded it because she knew what Josefa wanted to talk about, she said, "Of course. Shall we sit here in the sun?"

Josefa drew a chair up to the table under the jacaranda tree. "I know there's anger between Franco and Ricardo. My husband can be hard and sometimes he pushes too much, but it's because he wants Ricardo to be the best." She picked up a fallen jacaranda blossom off the table. "It's because he wants Ricardo to be what he himself couldn't be."

Her gaze met Megan's across the table. "Franco was good. He was the best. Then he was hurt, and after that he wasn't as good as he had been. But he tried. He fought Sunday after Sunday, pushing himself, trying so hard that it broke my heart. But what he had was gone. The corridas were few and far between, the towns smaller. And the people who came to see him fight..." Josefa shook her head. "Someone once said that the real beast at a bullfight is the crowd, and it's true.

"Finally the day came when Franco had to face the fact that it was time to end it. It was finished. The dream that he would be the best there had ever been had ended for him, but not for Ricardo. What he couldn't have himself he wanted for his son."

She looked at Megan from across the table. "Don't you see, Megan? He wants Ricardo to be what he couldn't be. That's why he pushes. That's why he was afraid when you and Ricardo married. He was afraid you would take away the dream he had for Ricardo."

"But is it Ricardo's dream?" And when Josefa didn't answer, Megan said, "I was afraid my fear would make him afraid, Josefa. Franco said..." She stopped and shook her head. "No, I won't blame it on Franco. It was me. I left Ricardo because I hated what he did, because I wasn't woman enough to let him be the man he had to be, the man he is today."

Her face was serious, sad. "I still hate what he does, and I'll still be afraid. But I'll hide my fear and I'll remember that he was a matador when I fell in love with him. That's who he is. I can't change it."

"And the love you have for each other hasn't changed. That's what you must remember."

"No," Megan said. "It hasn't changed." She hesitated. "I'll speak to Ricardo, Josefa. I'll ask him to make it up with his father."

"*Gracias*, Megan. And I'll speak to Franco. For all his faults he's a good man. I don't know what it is that happened between him and Ricardo. I only know that Franco can't sleep, that he paces our room like an angry bear and that he refuses to tell me what's wrong. It's a terrible thing when father and son quarrel. They'll have to work together this weekend. Ricardo will test the young bulls and the *beseras*, the cows, and Franco will record their abilities. Isabel and Fernando are coming, and we've invited other guests, as well. Afterward there will be a fiesta. It should be a happy time, Megan. I pray that it will be."

Megan got up, went around to the other side of the table and put her hand on Josefa's shoulder. "Don't worry. I'll talk to Ricardo."

He was in the shower when she went into their room, but as soon as he came out, she said, "You and your father can't go on this way, Ricardo. You have to make it up with him." His jaw firmed, but before he could say anything she continued, "This is upsetting to all of us, but especially to your mother and to Pilar." She went to her dressing table, picked up her brush and began to brush her hair. "He's still your father. He loves you and he wants what's best for you. If we're to live here until our house is built, we have to get along. If we can't, then I think we should look for a place in San Rafael."

"That wouldn't be practical," he said.

"No, it wouldn't." She turned and faced him. "The *tienta* is Saturday. That's the day after tomorrow. Your mother wants it to be a happy occasion, but it won't be unless you make it up with your father."

"All right," he said, "but if he doesn't treat you with courtesy, if he doesn't respect you as my wife, then it's over between us and we'll move into San Rafael."

"Please try to make it up with him," Megan said. "It's important for all of us."

That night at dinner Franco made the first move. "Juan has selected the cows," he told Ricardo. "I think you'll approve." He looked at Pilar. "One of them is small enough for you. If you want to, after the more serious business of the testing, I'll show you how to *torear.* Would you like to give it a try?"

"Would I?" She clapped her hands together.

"With your mother's permission, of course." Franco cleared his throat. "It's a calf," he said to Megan. "There's really no danger. I thought Pilar might enjoy it."

Megan nodded. "I'm sure she would."

Franco took a sip of his wine. "How are you feeling?"

"Better, thank you."

"Have you seen a doctor?"

"Yes, today."

"What did he say?" Ricardo asked.

Megan hesitated. She didn't want to lie, but neither did she want everyone at the table to know she was pregnant until she had told Ricardo. "He gave me some vitamins and told me to take it easy for a few days. It's the altitude. I'll be all right."

"You're sure there's nothing wrong?" Ricardo looked worried. "You're sure?"

"Nothing that time won't take care of." That much was true. In seven months she'd be perfectly fine.

The day was as bright and as beautiful as only a summer day in Mexico could be. Pilar knocked on Megan's bedroom door a little after eight, and they had breakfast together out in the secluded garden. But while Megan wanted to relax and enjoy the sun, Pilar was in a fever of impatience to be gone.

"Hurry up," she said again and again. "It's almost time for everything to start."

Megan smiled at her daughter, marveling at how well Pilar had adjusted to life in Mexico. With jeans stuffed into the new boots that Ricardo had had made for her, a blue-and-white-checked shirt and a wide-brimmed straw hat, she looked like a Mexican rancher's daughter, except for the long blond braid that hung down her back.

Finally, because Megan knew she couldn't hold her back any longer, she said, "Fernando and Isabel have the room next door. He's probably going to be leaving in a few minutes to go out to the *tentadero*, the family bullring. You can go with him if you promise not to get in the way and to do exactly what your father tells you to do."

"I promise!" Pilar threw her arms around her mother's neck and jumped up from the table. "See you later," she said, grabbing the straw hat from the chair next to her and running from the garden.

Megan took a leisurely shower, then she, too, dressed in jeans and boots. And she smiled, remembering that other *tienta* she'd gone to so long ago. That was the first time she had ever seen Ricardo. She had thought how tall and handsome he was, and she supposed, looking back on it, that she had fallen in love with him that very first day.

And thinking back to that day, she remembered that she hadn't been frightened at all, that she'd been almost as excited as Pilar had been today.

What had changed her? Had it been love, and if that was so, were love and fear inextricably bound? Did loving someone make you afraid for them, the way a mother was afraid when her child left home for the first time? When a daughter or a son went away to college? There came a time with children when you had to let go, when you had to learn to love with open hands.

But she hadn't done that with Ricardo. Because she loved him and feared for him, she hadn't loved with

open hands. She had shown no courage in the face of
her fear.

Megan sank down onto their bed and covered her
face with her hands. She wept for the years that her
fear had kept them apart, for all of the time they had
lost. And she resolved that she would change, that
from this day forward she would be the woman Ricardo wanted her to be. She would be strong for him
and for herself.

Chapter 15

When Megan and Isabel arrived in a pickup truck driven by one of the ranch hands, there were already people going up to the *palco*, the small gallery of seats with an arched tiled roof above one section of the ring.

When she got out of the truck, Megan stood for a moment and looked around her. The sky was a clear, clean blue. Hawthorn trees, winged elm, *huisache* trees and tall, spiny saguaro cactus grew in the pastureland where the brave bulls grazed, separated from the cows by high stone fences.

To the north were shadowed mountains. To the south, on a rise that looked out over the mountains and fields that were golden in the noonday sun, was the place where she and Ricardo would build their home.

Megan looked up at the hill and knew how it would be when they were there. The four of them, a family.

She laid her hand against her stomach and thought of the child she carried and hoped that it would be a boy.

"Come along," Isabel said. "Things will start soon." And together they climbed the stone steps up to the rows of seats.

Pilar was in the first row. She waved and said, "Hurry, Mom. Hurry, *Tía* Isabel. I saved these seats for you."

And though Megan would have preferred sitting farther back, she followed Isabel down to the first row of seats.

There were other guests, ranchers and aficionados, men who loved everything about the art of bullfighting, and a few women, dressed like Megan and Isabel in tailored pants or jeans and boots.

Below her she saw Ricardo, and she thought as she looked at him that he was even more handsome than the first time she had seen him. He had been wearing a *traje corto* then, as he was now, tight trousers with the short, tight jacket, this time in brown, with Spanish boots and a white linen shirt. And she remembered that she had thought how tall and slim he'd looked, how mysteriously foreign.

He stood near the *burladero,* the wooden shield built slightly out in front of the openings in the *barrera,* the heavy red fence that enclosed the ring, talking to his father and to two of the men who would be helping today. He said something to Franco, and Franco nodded, then turned and came up to the *palco* to take his place in front of a flat stone ledge that held the book in which he would record the qualifications of the bulls and cows that would be tested. He looked over at Isabel and Megan and said, "*Buenos días.* It will start soon."

"May I stand next to you, Grandfather?" Pilar asked.

"Yes," he said. "But you must be very quiet."

"I will be," she whispered.

He looked down into the ring. "Are you ready?" he asked Ricardo.

"Ready." Ricardo smiled up at Isabel and Megan.

"*Suerte,*" Isabel said.

"Yes, *suerte,* Ricardo." Megan threw him a kiss. *Suerte,* my love.

A picador, whose job it would be to pic the bull from horseback with a lance, stationed himself at the side of the ring opposite the *puerta del toril,* the door from which the animals would come.

Franco opened the book. He turned and looked at the gathered guests. "We will begin," he said. "*Silencio, por favor,* and please do not move around." Then he said, "*Puerta,*" and a man below took a long, hooked pole and opened the door where a young bull that had been separated from the rest of the bulls waited.

"This is number forty-three," the man below said.

The door opened. The young bull exploded into the ring, stopped for a fraction of a second to get its bearings, then dashed straight at the padded horse.

The picador jabbed in the lance, but the bull wouldn't back away. He charged again and again.

"You see how good he is," Isabel whispered. "How brave."

"But he's bleeding," Megan whispered back. "He's hurt."

"The wounds aren't deep. They'll be attended to and he'll heal. Now watch. Ricardo will draw him away with his body but not with the cape because fighting bulls must never see the cape until they're in the plaza. They have an extraordinary intuition. They learn and they never forget, and once they've learned they'll charge the body, not the cape."

Ricardo and the men helping him drew the first bull out of the ring. Another took its place, and another. And when the testing of the bulls was finished, he began to test the cows.

"The brave ones will be used for breeding," Isabel said. "They can be as dangerous, sometimes even more dangerous than a bull."

A cow rushed into the ring, thin, razor-sharp horns glinting in the sun. She raced toward the horse, was given a pic, charged again and received another small, carefully placed jab.

Ricardo stepped from behind the *burladero,* holding the magenta-and-yellow cape in front of him. "Aha!" he called. The cow turned and raced toward him.

There was silence in the *palco.* The only sounds were the rush of hooves against the earth and the soft "Aha! Aha!"

"Now he's testing for style, to see how the animal will attack and how it follows the cape," Isabel whispered. "See how the cow is beginning to follow where he leads?"

"Dos capatazos," Franco said softly.

Ricardo brought the cow closer, and yet closer. And perfect animal that she was, she followed his every movement.

The next cow to come out was as good, but the third cow was difficult and dangerous. She attacked the padded horse, slamming hard, unmindful of the sting of the pic, and when Ricardo tried to lure her away, she attacked him hard and fast, ignoring the cape, going after his body.

He tried a veronica, but as he passed the cow, the animal stopped, jerked its head up and tried to drive its horns into Ricardo's legs. And she would have if Ricardo hadn't been quick.

On and on it went. He brought the cow closer and still closer, making it do what he wanted it to do.

The breath caught in Megan's throat, and she was afraid for him. Then she remembered that Pilar, too, was witnessing this dangerous moment, and she looked to where her daughter stood beside her grandfather, fearful that if anything happened, if a horn caught Ricardo again...

But Pilar, though her small body was stiff with tension, didn't look afraid. Small hands clasped together, she watched her father with an intensity and an understanding that seemed far beyond her years.

She's strong, Megan thought. As strong as her father, as her grandfather. And for a moment the old anger came back because this was just a business to Franco. He'd seen this so many times before. He wasn't afraid. He expected this of Ricardo. Then she looked at Franco and her anger faded because she saw in him the same gut-twisting fear she felt. His face was white. He clutched the stone edge of the *palco*, and his lips moved with the whispered words *"Cuidado, hijo mío.* Be careful my boy."

And suddenly she knew how afraid he was, how afraid he had always been.

"¡Ya!" he called out. "Enough!"

"No," Ricardo said without looking up. "She'll do more."

And it went on until at last he motioned to the two assistants behind the *burladero,* and they rushed into the ring to help get the cow out.

At last, when the serious work of the *tienta* was finished, it was time for whatever guests might want a chance at smaller, less dangerous cows. Fernando took a turn, as did most of the male guests and one or two of the women.

At the end a calf was brought in, and Pilar was given a red serge muleta that wasn't as heavy as the magenta-and-yellow cape. Her grandfather showed her how to hold it.

"Like this," he said. "When the animal runs toward you, move it to your side, away from your body."

"I know! I know! I watched Dad. I can do it."

They brought the calf in. Pilar waved the red cloth. "Aha!" she cried, as her father had done, and the animal, head down, charged.

She stood her ground and waited until the last moment to swing the cloth and pass it past her body.

"*¡Olé!*" Ricardo cried. "That was beautiful!"

She turned to smile at him, and when she did, the calf turned back to charge, caught her in the midsection and bounced her backward. Franco grabbed the calf and held it while Ricardo helped Pilar up.

She pulled away from her father, glared at the little animal, picked up the straw hat that had fallen to the ground, slapped it on her head and picked up the red cloth.

And she stood there, a ferocious frown on her small face, playing him until her father said, "That's enough, Pilar," and one of the helpers took the animal away.

"You did well," Franco told her when they walked out to where the pickups and the Jeeps were parked. "I'm proud of you."

Pilar grinned up at him, then said to her mother, "Were you scared, Mom?"

Megan shook her head and, looking over Pilar's head to Franco, she said, "No, I wasn't scared. I knew your grandfather was taking care of you."

Franco's dark eyebrows shot up. He started to say something, hesitated, then took a handkerchief out of his pocket and wiped it across his face. "Your dad's going to be busy here for a while," he told Pilar. "Your Aunt Isabel will ride back with Fernando, so you and your mother come with me in the pickup."

They walked out to where the vehicles were parked. He picked Pilar up and put her inside, then he took Megan's hand. "Let me help you," he said.

And Megan knew, though it was only a small gesture, that they had taken the first tentative step toward a better understanding.

That night the warm summer air was as soft as a baby's kiss. Lanterns had been strung all across the flower-filled patio, and candles shone from every table. A group of mariachis played near the old stone fountain, and at the far end of the patio two long tables of food and drink had been set up.

There was crisp roast pork, Mexican rice, black beans, meat-filled empanadas, country ham, hot tortillas, white country cheese and salsa hot enough to bring tears to the eyes of the bravest of men. At the other table a bartender filled crystal glasses with red or white wine or goblets of sangria.

The women guests had changed into summer party dresses, the men to trousers and jackets. Megan wore a long pale blue gown, typically Mexican with wide ruffles around the off-the-shoulder top and down the length of the full skirt. She had pulled her hair back off her face and fastened it in the back with a cluster of forget-me-nots.

She felt festive, full of life and love tonight because, of all the places in the world, this was where she wanted to be. When it came to having a party, there wasn't anybody in the world who could do it quite as well as the Mexicans. The economy might be bad, there might be problems to face tomorrow, but when it came to a celebration, everything else was forgotten in the warmth of their friends, the music, the wine and the food. She had been right to come back. This was where she belonged—here in Ricardo's homeland.

He was the center of attention tonight, surely the most handsome man there, filled with confidence because the day had been good. He smiled at the women who flirted with him, but it was Megan whose gaze he sought. And each time his eyes met hers across the patio with a look that said, "Soon, my Meggie, we'll be together in our bed," her body grew warm with desire.

As the evening went on, she danced with some of the guests, then with Fernando. When the dance was finished, Fernando said, "Let's see if we can pry that husband of yours away from his bullfight buddies." And he led her to the table where Ricardo sat with a group of men.

Ricardo smiled up at her and pulled out a chair so that she could sit next to him, but his attention was focused on the talk going on around him.

They talked about the bulls, the good ones, the dangerous ones. They spoke of the quality of the young bulls and cows they had seen today, of last week's corridas, and of the corridas yet to come.

"Ricardo will be number one again," they said. "You'll see when he fights in Mexico City next week."

"He's not one to let a goring stop him," a man said.

"You are *mucho hombre*," another said.

They raised their glasses to drink to him. "You're the best there is," they said.

Pilar came to stand between Megan and Ricardo. She listened to the talk for a little while, then yawned and leaned her head against her father's shoulder.

"It's late," Megan said. "You'd better get to bed. I'll take you in."

"No," Ricardo said. "I'll take her."

And when Pilar told the others good-night, and kissed Megan, Ricardo took her hand and went into the house with her.

The men at the table continued to talk of the bulls. They told of the matadors who had been gored, and of the men who had died in the ring. They spoke of Joselito, who had been so sure the bulls would never get him; of Manolete, killed on the final thrust of his sword by the bull Islero; of Alberto Balderas, who died trying to help another matador; and of the handsome young Pacquiri, who had bled to death before he could reach the hospital.

Megan sat as though frozen. She looked at the faces of the men who spoke and remembered that the first time she had seen Ricardo she had thought of him as a gladiator, a gladiator facing death in the arena. She knew she hadn't been wrong.

Next Sunday these men who talked so easily of bravery and of death would be in the front row of the Plaza Mexico, safely above the danger that Ricardo and the other two matadors would face. They would applaud and shout their *¡Olés!* and grow silent when the matador brought the bull close and ever closer to his slim, vulnerable body.

She remembered the wound she had seen when Ricardo lay helpless in the hospital, and she wanted to shout at them that there was nothing beautiful or romantic about this spectacle where death was the final victor.

But she said nothing. She sat in quiet desperation, hands folded in her lap, her face expressionless, and tried to hide the sickness of her fear. She had vowed that never again would she try to stop Ricardo from doing what he wanted to do. She would keep that vow, but, oh, there was a part of her that wanted to take him away from here to where there were no brave bulls, no cheering crowds, no arena of sand where he would stand alone to face his enemy.

Ricardo came back to the table. He took Megan's hand and said, "Excuse us, gentlemen," and led her to a secluded section of the patio. "I'm sorry I was gone so long," he murmured as he took her in his arms and they began to dance. "I wanted to be sure Pilar was asleep. Were you all right? What did the men talk about?"

"The bulls," she said.

"I'm sorry, *querida.* Were you bored?"

"No, I wasn't bored." She moved closer into his arms.

"It's been a good day, hasn't it?"

"Yes." Megan looked up at him. "You must be tired."

"No." He laughed. "No, I feel wonderful. The *tienta* was a success, the animals were good, and it's a beautiful night for a fiesta. My family and my friends are here. Pilar's safely tucked in her bed and you're in my arms. What more could a man want, Megan?"

He stopped dancing, and when she looked up at him, he kissed her. His mouth tasted of cool white wine. She clung to him, parting her lips under his, holding him as he held her. She didn't ever want to let him go; she wanted to keep him here where he was safe. And for a moment her fear was so great that she almost said, "Don't! Please don't do it anymore because I can't stand it. Because you're my life and I would die if anything happened to you."

But she didn't say the words. She pressed her mouth to his, and when he let her go, she was able to smile and say, "You taste like wine."

He smiled back. "You didn't have any wine tonight. Don't you feel well?"

"I feel fine."

The mariachis began to play another Mexican waltz. Ricardo held Megan away from him, then he bowed from his waist and said, "May I have this waltz, Señora Montoya?"

"I've been saving it just for you, Señor Montoya."

He kissed her hand. "Has anyone told you that you're the most beautiful woman here tonight?"

"No, *señor*, but you should know because you've certainly looked at all of them."

He pretended to frown as he drew her into his arms. "But there's only one that I'm interested in. Tonight when we're alone I plan to show her just how interested." He put his hand against the small of her back and pressed her close. "Very interested."

"¡Señor!" She stepped away, and with eyebrows raised asked, "Is that a weapon you're carrying in your trousers?"

He laughed, and it was a good sound. "I love you. I love the way you look, the way you feel in my arms. I love that unexpected bawdiness. I love everything about you." He drew her close again, and they began to dance to the music of the waltz.

The blue ruffled Mexican dress whirled around her slim ankles, and one by one the flowers that had bound her hair came loose and cascaded over her bare shoulders.

"Mañana, cuando ya estás lejos," the marchias sang.

"Cuando ya estás sola, me recordarás,
Tus labios, ansierán mis besos,
Tus ojos por mi llorarán.
Tomorrow, when you are far away,
When you are alone, remember me.
Your lips, answering my kisses,
Your eyes, weeping for me . . ."

It was a lovely song, a beautifully romantic song.

When the dance ended, Ricardo drew her back into the shadows so that he could kiss her again. "You're so lovely," he said when he let her go. "So unbelievably mine."

She knew then that it was time to tell him her news. When he let her go, she said, "I have something to tell you, Ricardo. I'm afraid I lied to you the other day."

"Lied?" Ricardo shook his head. "I don't understand. About what?"

"About the doctor. About what he said."

His face went still. He gripped her arms. "What is it? Are you ill? What—"

"I am . . ." The tip of her tongue touched her upper lip. "I'm pregnant, Ricardo."

"Preg—" His eyes widened. He swallowed hard. "Pregnant?"

Her lips quivered in an uncertain smile. "I hope you're pleased."

"Pleased!" He took a deep, shaking breath. "Oh, Meggie," he whispered. "Meggie."

Her face was touched by moonlight, and he knew he had never seen anyone as beautiful as she was in that moment. She was his wife and his lover, the mother of the child they had and of the child to come. He loved her more than he had ever thought it possible to love.

He drew her into his arms and held her close. "Meggie," he whispered against her hair. "My Meggie."

They lay side by side in bed that night. He touched her breasts and said, "They've grown fuller. I should have noticed." He began to kiss her there, gently, tenderly. "Tell me if I hurt you."

She laced her fingers through his fine dark hair. "You never hurt me."

"Soon our child will nestle here." He raised himself on one elbow and looked down at her. "Are you sure you're all right? There's no danger?"

Megan shook her head. "There's no danger. I'm only thirty-one. I could have a half dozen more."

"Oh, no, you couldn't!" He placed his hand over her stomach. "How many months along are you?"

"Almost three. If my calculations are right, it happened that weekend on the boat."

"Your fault," he said.

"My fault?"

"For making me crazy with wanting you." He felt himself grow hard and moved a little away from her.

"What is it?" she asked, sensing his withdrawal. "What's the matter?"

"I don't want to hurt you. I mean, maybe we shouldn't—"

"Yes, we should." She drew him closer and began to stroke him. "Yes, we should," she said against his lips.

"If you're sure."

"I'm sure."

"Well, then…" He rolled over onto his back. "I'm ready."

Megan stared down at him. "Yes, you certainly are."

"Hop aboard."

But for a moment she waited, smiling down at him, for this was the man she loved with all her heart, the father of Pilar, and of the child who was just beginning to grow, the child he had placed deep inside her.

She straddled his hips and slowly lowered herself over him. "I love you."

"Ah, Megan." He reached up and began to stroke her breasts. "My love. My dearest love."

Then there were no words, only the slow, steady movement of body against body. He grasped her hips, she held his shoulders, and together they moved to a rhythm as old as time.

He watched her, the grace of her movements, the head that went back when the excitement grew, the splay of golden hair over her bare shoulders, the delicate line of her throat, the full, peaked breasts. He spanned her still-slender waist and reached to cup her bottom to help her move against him.

He said, "More, love. Oh, yes, Meggie. More. Oh, more."

And in that final moment when he knew he could no longer stand this sweet torture, when he knew passion had gripped her as it had gripped him, and she whispered small anguished words of pleasure and completion, he cried her name, "Meggie! Oh, Meggie!" and climbed with her to the almost unbearable heights of their shared passion.

It was only later, when he slept with his body curled tightly to hers, that she remembered what his friends had said tonight about the men who had died in the ring.

She remembered all of their names: Joselito, Balderas, Monolete, Pacquiri.

And she remembered that in a week Ricardo would face the most dangerous bulls in Mexico.

Chapter 16

"We have a wonderful secret to tell you," Megan told Pilar the next morning when the three of them were having breakfast in the small garden off their bedroom. "Your dad and I are happy about it, and we think you will be, too."

"A secret?" Pilar, who had just bitten into a slice of mango, looked up. "What? What is it?"

"We're going to have a baby."

"A baby?" Her eyes went wide with surprise. "We're going to have a baby? When? When's it coming?"

"In the spring. In April."

"That's what we could call her if it's a girl!" So excited that she bounced up and down on her chair, Pilar said, "I'm going to have a sister! Or a brother! What do you think it'll be? I'd really like a sister, but it would be sorta nice to have a brother, wouldn't it?"

"Yes, it would." Ricardo smiled across the table at her. "But I'm pretty partial to girls, especially to one particular girl."

Pilar laughed. "Me!"

"Yes, you."

"Having a new baby is a lot of work," Megan said. "I'm going to need help taking care of it."

"I'll help you, Mom. I'm almost eight. There's a lot I can do." She looked at her mother. "Where are we going to get it from?"

"From in here." Megan put her hand on her stomach. "In a few months my stomach's going to grow bigger and you'll be able to feel the baby."

Pilar looked awestruck. "It's in there?"

Megan nodded. "Just like you were."

"Did you know about that, Dad?"

Ricardo smiled. "Yes, I knew."

"Are we going to tell Grandmother and Grandfather?"

Ricardo poured hot chocolate into her cup. "We'll tell them tonight at dinner. Do you think you can keep it a secret until then?"

"Sure." She looked thoughtful. "If it's a boy, what are we going to name him?"

"I don't know," Megan said. "When the time comes, you can help us decide."

"Willie Bob's a nice name."

Ricardo coughed and spilled his coffee. And Megan said, "It doesn't go very well with Montoya, but we'll certainly think about it, Pilar."

Ricardo pushed his chair back. "I've got a lot of work to do this morning, so I'll see the two of you later." He kissed Megan, then Pilar. "Remember," he cautioned, "it's a secret until tonight."

"I'll remember," she said.

But all that day Pilar was in a fever of impatience, and by dinner time she could hardly contain herself. As soon as they sat down at the table, she said, "Tell 'em, Mom."

Josefa looked up. "Tell us what."

Ricardo took Megan's hand. "Megan is pregnant."

"Pregnant?" Josefa's face lighted up. "Oh, my dear, I'm so pleased. That's wonderful news! When will it be?"

"In April," Megan said.

"Well, now..." Franco raised his wineglass. "Congratulations. I'm happy for both of you." But he didn't look happy when he turned to Ricardo and said, "Does that mean you'll go to Spain alone?"

"Spain?" Megan looked from Franco to Ricardo. "What does he mean?"

"I'm scheduled to fight at the April fair in Sevilla," Ricardo said. "Then in Málaga and Madrid."

"You didn't tell me."

"Dad only made the arrangements a few days ago, Megan. It wasn't definite until today." He tried to smile, but he knew from her expression that this had come as a shock. "I was saving it for a surprise, *querida*. I thought we could make it a second honeymoon."

"It will be a short season," Franco said. "Ricardo will be back by the end of June."

The end of June? Devastated, Megan could only look at Ricardo. All she could think about was that he wasn't going to be here when his new son or daughter was born. And that she wouldn't be able to go to Spain with him because it would be too near her time.

"I didn't know about the baby," he said. "I'm sorry. If you want me to, I'll cancel Spain."

"Cancel Spain!" Franco started up out of his chair. "Don't be ridiculous. You're scheduled to fight with Galán in Sevilla. Then with Manzanares and possibly with Niño de la Capea. All of the top matadors in Spain, Ricardo. It's a wonderful opportunity. You can't back out."

"Megan will be all right with us," Josefa said. "You know that we'll look after her, Ricardo."

"Yes, I know, but..." He looked at Megan. She sat very still, her face expressionless.

"It's your profession," she said quietly. "It's what you do. I understand."

She barely touched her food, and when dessert was served, she said, "Will you excuse me? I'm a little tired tonight."

Ricardo stood to help her up. "I'll come with you."

But Megan shook her head. "I'm going to read for a little while, then go to sleep."

She kissed Pilar and said good-night to Josefa and Franco. As she turned away, she heard Franco say, "There will be two fights in Sevilla, maybe three. From there you'll go to..."

She went down the long, arched corridor that led to the bedrooms. Last night there had been moonlight, but tonight there were shadows on the moon and a chill in the air. She was cold. She should have worn a sweater. She...

"Oh, God!" she whispered and, holding herself as though in pain, she leaned against the cold stone wall. She felt bereft, empty and alone, helpless because nothing had changed. It was as it had been eight years ago, as it would be eight years from now. She loved

Ricardo, and no matter what happened she would never leave him again. But it would be so much harder than she had thought it would be.

She didn't want to have this baby alone; she wanted him with her, wanted him to share in the joy of that first moment when she held their baby in her arms. She needed him, needed his strength.

She remembered the time he had been gored in Spain. If that happened this time, she wouldn't be with him. He would be alone, as she would be alone.

And there wasn't anything she could do about it.

Megan didn't attend the corrida in Mexico City the following Sunday. Ricardo had asked her if she wanted to go, and when she said she didn't, he didn't press her. He knew they had to talk about Spain, but every time he brought it up she changed the subject.

Work on their house was scheduled to start. They had seen, and with a few minor changes, had approved the architect's plans. It was to be of Spanish colonial design, with most of the rooms opening on to a central patio. There would be five bedrooms, a living room, a formal dining room, a breakfast room, a large kitchen and a combination den and library.

It was to be their dream house, their home on a hill overlooking the low, rolling hills, the fields of wildflowers and the distant mountains.

Whenever Ricardo brought up the subject of the coming fight in Mexico City or the April trip to Spain, she began to talk about the house. Should all of the walls be white? she would ask. What about Pilar's room? Shouldn't that be more colorful? And what about the patio? She wanted a central fountain with flowers and plants. And roses. Lots of roses.

And though Ricardo knew Spain was something they needed to talk about, he didn't press the subject. Perhaps the baby would come earlier than Megan anticipated and she and the baby could go with him. Or perhaps she could join him in Spain.

He hated the idea of not being with her when their baby was born, and of being separated from her for almost three months, but he didn't know what to do about it. Spain was important to him. It was important to his career.

On the Sunday morning of the corrida in Mexico City he got up early. "Dad and Larrea and I will have breakfast in Mexico City," he told Megan. "I want to go to the *sorteo,* the choosing of the bulls at eleven."

He sat on the side of the bed next to her. "Isabel and Fernando will be going. Are you sure you don't want to go with them?"

"No, I . . . I'm probably going to see the architect today."

"Well, then . . ." He kissed her. "I'll be back tonight."

"Have a good day," she said. "Break a leg."

He looked startled. "What?"

"Break a leg." Megan smiled. "I'm sorry. It's something you say to theater people before they go onstage. But I guess you don't say it to a matador."

"Not unless you want a taste of the sword." He kissed her again. "Go back to sleep if you can."

"I will. *Suerte,* darling."

"*Gracias,* Megan. Until tonight then."

Megan didn't go back to sleep after he left. She put a robe on, and though the morning was cold, she opened the French doors and went out into the garden. Today the man she loved, armed only with a piece of cloth and a toothpick-like sword that would only be used in that last desperate moment of truth, would face a thousand-pound animal that had been bred to fight. He would stand alone in the arena, like the men of ancient Crete, or the gladiators who had fought in Rome's Colosseum. He would call the animal to him and pit himself, his fragile man's body, against a killer beast.

She could hide her fear from Ricardo, but she couldn't hide it from herself. She was paralyzed by it, sickened and shaken by it.

When Pilar came to get her for breakfast, Megan told her to go have breakfast with her grandmother. "I'm a little tired this morning. I'll have something later."

But it was almost noon when she left her room, and when she did, she found Pilar on the patio, looking worried and forlorn. "Where's your grandmother?" Megan asked.

"In the chapel," Pilar answered in a subdued voice. "She had on a black dress and one of those black lace things over her head."

"A mantilla," Megan said.

"Uh-huh. And she looked really upset, Mom. Did she go into the chapel because it's Sunday?"

"Because it's Sunday and probably because she wanted to say a special prayer for your dad."

"Do you think it would be all right if we went in with her? If we said a prayer for Dad, too? Do you think she'd mind?"

"No, honey, I think she'd like us to." Megan took Pilar's hand, and together they went out and down the cobblestone path that led to the small family chapel.

It was cool inside, lit by the sun that filtered in through two stained glass windows and by the glow of votive candles. It was a small chapel, meant only for the family. There were three short pews. Josefa was in the first, on her knees, facing the altar, her face half-hidden by hands clasped in prayer.

Pilar, her small face solemn, looked up at Megan, and when Megan nodded, she slid into the pew next to her grandmother.

Josefa turned her head, and Megan, who had followed Pilar into the pew, saw the glistening tears in the older woman's eyes. Josefa took Pilar's hand and kissed her fingertips. "Come," she whispered. "Let us say a prayer for your father."

And the three who loved him knelt together and prayed for his safety.

His first bull was almost perfect. He worked it well with the cape, first with a series of veronicas, then with a media-veronica, a flowing lance that he used to end the series and which brought the crowd to its feet.

The pic was good, and because the bull was an exceptionally fine animal and because the crowd demanded it, Ricardo decided to do the banderillas himself. He cited the bull, calling, *"¡Aha, toro! ¡Aha!"* Then, holding the banderillas at the level of his shoulder, he ran in a quarter circle toward the animal, cutting in across the bull's charge. When the bull lowered its head to hook, Ricardo brought his feet together, raised the banderillas high and, as he passed the horns, plunged the sticks into the hump of neck muscle and pivoted away.

It was all right on the first two parts, but on the third, just as he began his zigzag run, he stumbled and almost fell. Before his helpers could run to his aid he steadied himself, began his run again, planted the sticks and danced away from the bull.

When he went to the fence, his father said, "*¿Qué pasa?* Why did you stumble?"

"There was something on the sand."

But there hadn't been anything on the sand. A sudden trembling, a weakness in his legs had made him falter. That scared the hell out of him because strong legs were as important to a matador as knowledge, grace and bravery. He had to be able to spin away at that final moment, had to position his legs just so. If the legs went, there was nothing left.

A trumpet sounded, signaling the final act of the drama. His father handed him his sword and muleta. With his *montera,* the traditional black hat all matadors wore, in his hand, Ricardo walked to just below the box where the president of the corrida sat to ask permission to begin the final act. When it was given, he turned back to the ring and handed the *montera* to Larrea. Then, motioning his helpers behind the fence, he began to work the bull.

He started with an *ayudado por alto,* both hands positioned in front of him, provoking the charge, absolutely still, then moving his hands slightly away from his body as the bull charged past him.

He did pass after pass and tried not to think of the weakness in his legs. But the fear was there, fear that if he didn't end this soon he might stumble again and fall.

When it was time for the moment of truth, that final moment when the matador must risk his life to deliver the sword thrust, he tried not to think about his legs. He positioned his animal, and when the moment came, he thrust the sword in straight and true, barely managing to pivot out of reach of the deadly horns.

They awarded him two ears. He made a circle of the ring amid showers of carnations and roses, *botas* of wine, sombreros and one or two ladies' high-heeled shoes.

"It went well," his father said when he returned to stand behind the *barrera*. "Bravo, Ricardo!"

Ricardo leaned on the heavy red wooden fence. *"Gracias,"* he murmured.

Another bull ran into the ring, and his father turned to watch.

"Is it your legs, Matador?" Larrea asked in a low voice. "Do they trouble you?"

"No." Ricardo looked at his trainer, then away. "Of course not," he said, because there was in him the notion that if he didn't give voice to the problem, it would go away. Therefore he would deny it as long as he could. He was a little tired. He needed a rubdown and a good night's sleep. That was all.

Luis Gomez, the matador who followed him, fought well and true, but when it came time to kill the bull, his luck turned bad. The crowd jeered. They whistled and threw their pillows down at him.

The third matador, Pepe Alvarez, had a bad and cowardly bull. He did the best he could with it, which the crowd couldn't understand, and killed it quickly, which they hated.

It was time for Ricardo's second bull. He thought his legs would be better now because he had rested, and they were, until halfway through the faena. He felt the weakness then, and it made him angry. He did pass after pass, then killed quickly and cleanly and left the arena with cries of "Mon-to-ya! Mon-to-ya!"

On the way back to the hotel, because he had little to say, his father said, "You're tired. That's to be expected. This was your first corrida in almost five months. You did well. You'll do even better next week."

Next week.

The lobby was crowded with well-wishers, and some of them came up to the suite Franco had taken so that Ricardo could change. Ricardo stayed with them for a few minutes, then motioned to his father to talk to them while he bathed and changed.

Larrea, who had followed him into the bedroom, said, "You look tired, Matador. When you've had your shower, I'll give you a massage."

Another of his cuadrilla came in to help him out of his suit of lights, and when that was done, Ricardo went in to shower. As soon as he came out, he lay on the portable table Larrea had set up and Larrea began the massage.

Ricardo tried to relax, tried not to think of today's corrida, or next Sunday's, or of the Sunday after that. Or of the trip to Spain when he would have to leave Meggie. He tried very hard to separate his professional thoughts from his feelings about her, but he couldn't because she was so inextricably bound to everything he did, to every phase, to every part of his life.

She had told him this morning that she didn't want to come to the corrida today because she might see the architect. He hadn't believed her. He knew she had used the architect as an excuse because she didn't want to see him fight again.

But he would keep fighting for as long as he could. He didn't want to hurt her, but this was what he did. It was all that he knew.

The afternoon had taken a lot out of him. He was bone weary and his muscles ached.

"You're tense," Larrea said. "Relax."

He wished that he could.

"You fight a *mano a mano* with Felipe Guzman next week," Larrea said.

"Yes."

"Is he as good as he thinks he is?"

"He's good."

"But you're better."

"And older." Ten years older. Guzman was twenty-three. Eager, hungry to be the best.

"Age means nothing," Larrea said, though they both knew that wasn't true.

He covered Ricardo with a clean white sheet. "Later I'll send down for something to eat," he said. "What would you like?"

"Nothing, *gracias*. I'll eat later with my family."

"Then rest, Matador. You're tired."

Yes, Ricardo thought. I am tired.

He had called Megan from the hotel, and she was waiting for him when he got back to the ranch.

"I saw the corrida on television," she said, although she had watched for less than ten minutes. "You were wonderful."

"Gracias, mujer." He put his arms around her. "It's good to be home. I don't like being away from you, even for a day."

"Nor do I like your being away." She touched his face. "You look so tired."

"I am, a little."

"Your mother and Pilar have eaten and Pilar's gone to bed. I thought you and I could eat in our room, if that's all right with you."

"It's more than all right."

Megan put her arm around his waist, and together they crossed the patio and went down the corridor that led to their room. While he changed into pajamas and a robe she went into the kitchen to get the dinner she had prepared earlier—a breast of chicken with wild rice, a vegetable salad, and a bottle of red wine, for him.

She thought he looked very tired, and though she knew he'd had a long day, his tiredness worried her. But what worried her even more was that when he turned to go into the bathroom he had been limping.

When she went back to their room, she arranged their plates on the table in front of the French doors.

"This looks good," he said. "I'm hungry."

"You should have eaten earlier."

"No, I wanted to eat with you." He saluted her with his glass. "What time did the architect come?"

"Actually..." Megan hesitated. "Actually he didn't. He said that something had come up."

"I see."

"We'll see him tomorrow."

"I'll be with Larrea tomorrow, practicing."

"Maybe you should rest instead, Ricardo. You've had a hard day. You—"

"No!" he said sharply. "I need to work tomorrow. The *mano a mano* is next week. I have to be ready."

"I understand." Megan looked down at her plate. "How did your legs feel today?"

"My legs?" He frowned, and she knew she shouldn't have asked. "They're fine," he said.

She cut a small piece of chicken and tried to think of something to make his angry look go away. "Your mother is teaching Pilar how to knit."

"Oh?" He looked puzzled.

"Baby clothes," she said.

"That's nice." He pushed his plate away. "I'm sorry. I'm not very hungry."

"That's all right." Megan stood up and began to clear the plates away. "I'll just take these back to the kitchen. And I'll look in on Pilar on the way back."

He kissed her. "The dinner was nice. I'm sorry I don't feel like eating."

"It doesn't matter." She smiled up at him, then took the tray and went out of the room. By the time she returned, he was in bed, turned away from the lamp on her side, seemingly asleep.

She undressed and got into bed beside him. He didn't move, but Megan knew he was awake. She rested her hand on his thigh, not in passion, but to reassure him that she was with him. And at last his breathing evened and he slept.

A little before dawn she felt his hands on her, and when she stirred, he said, "Megan?" She heard the need in his voice and turned into his arms.

He made love to her with an almost frantic urgency. When it was over and she made as though to move away, he said, "No, stay like this, sleep like this." He rested his head against the hollow of her shoulder. "Stay with me," he whispered.

And slept again.

Chapter 17

The corridas in both Mexico City and Guadalajara were outstanding successes. After the *mano a mano* with Felipe Guzman, the newspapers all over Mexico had carried the headlines: Guzman Does Well. Montoya Is Indisputably the Best!

Guzman would be one of the six vying for the Golden Sword, along with Arturo Cruz, Enrique Alcazar, Curro Mejias and Vicente Cano. They were all capable matadors, at the very top of their profession. The bulls were from Santacilia, a ranch whose bulls were known for their strength and bravery.

It would be the last corrida of the season, and Ricardo was glad. He wanted to rest and spend time with Megan before he went to Spain. If he couldn't be with her when the baby was born, at least he could be here during her pregnancy.

The night before the Estoque de Oro the family gathered for a pre-celebration dinner. They were festive and dressed for the occasion: Dōna Josefa in her finest black dress; Isabel in deep red that showed off the sparkle of her dark eyes; and Megan in the same blue dress she had worn the night after the _tienta_.

Ricardo had heard that pregnant women had a special glow, and it was true. He had never seen her looking quite as beautiful as she did tonight. When she leaned across the table to say something to Isabel, a strand of her hair caressed her cheek. He wanted to touch her, to enfold her in his arms and tell her how much he loved her, how much she meant to him. She and Pilar and the baby that would come in the spring.

He knew he had been quiet and withdrawn lately, and he knew Megan didn't understand and had been hurt by his silences. But he felt such pressure, such an overpowering need to prove to himself and to the fans who came to see him _torear_ that he was as good as he had been before the goring. He _had_ to be ready for this final competition of the season; he _had_ to be the best that he could be.

And there was a part of him that hated Juan Larrea every time he said, "You're not moving as quickly as you should, Ricardo. The legs are still weak. I'm worried."

"My legs are fine," he always insisted. And prayed that it was true.

He was in good physical shape, stronger than ever. His weight was a trim one-sixty, nearly all of it muscle. The stomach wound had healed and his belly was flat and hard. He was as good as he had been at twenty-three.

Guzman's age.

If it weren't for his legs . . .

He looked around the table at the faces of the people he loved—his sister and his mother, his father. He didn't want to disappoint his father. His dear Megan. Pilar.

"I'm going to sit right in the front row," his daughter announced. "In the middle, so I can see everything."

"You and your mother and Isabel and Fernando have the best seats in the plaza," Ricardo said. He smiled gently at his mother. "Are you sure you don't want to go, *Mamácita?*"

Josefa smiled back at him. "No, my son. But I'll be here when you return and we'll have another dinner to celebrate your success."

He should have known better than to have asked; his mother had never seen him fight. Most wives and mothers of the matadors he knew didn't attend the corridas. He was glad that Megan, without his asking, had said she would go tomorrow.

After dinner, when they moved into the living room for coffee, Pilar came to sit next to him. He put his arm around her, and when the hour grew late, she dozed against his shoulder.

"You'd better wake her so she can go to bed," Megan said.

He rubbed his chin across the top of his daughter's silky head. "No, let her stay. I'll carry her in later."

He gazed around the room at his family—his mother and father, his sister and her husband, his beloved Megan. I have so much, he thought. So much more than I ever hoped to have.

He loved the ranch where he had grown up, and this room with the big stone fireplace, the eighteenth-century painting of the Ascension that hung above it, the thick, dark Mexican rug, the heavy furniture, the clay pot of marigolds his mother had placed on the old carved coffee table between the two Remington bronzes. All of it so dear, so familiar. He would always be a part of the ranch, as it would still be a part of him. Even when he and Megan moved into their own home, he would be a part of the life here. And when his days as a matador were over, he would raise brave bulls with his father. Bulls for other men to fight.

When the hour grew late, his father said, "We'd better go to bed and rest now, Ricardo. We have to drive into Mexico City early so that we can go to the *sorteo* tomorrow. We should have spent the night there. You would have had more rest then."

But Ricardo shook his head. "No, I wanted to spend the night here with my family."

He stood and went to his mother. He kissed her, then Isabel, who seemed surprised by his unexpected display of affection, and picked Pilar up in his arms. She stirred but didn't awaken. He kissed the top of her head. "Come along, *muchachita,*" he said softly.

Megan said her good-nights and went ahead of him to open Pilar's door. He placed his child on the bed and helped hold her while Megan undressed her, and together they tucked her in. When Megan snapped off the bedside light, they stood with their arms around each other, looking down at their child.

"She's so beautiful," said softly. "She's a part of our love."

He wanted to hold on to this moment. He wanted it to always be like this, he and his wife and his child, an entity unto themselves, safe, indestructible.

They went back to their room. They showered together, and when they came out, he took a big white towel and carefully dried her. And while she stood he rested his head against her stomach where their baby grew. "I love you," he said to their unborn child. He raised his head. "And I love you, Megan. Always and forever."

He began to make love to her there. He caressed her with his hands and with his mouth, and when it became too much, he took her hand and led her to their bed.

They made love, hotly, sweetly, and when it was over, she went to sleep in his arms.

But it was a long time that night before Ricardo slept. He thought of tomorrow, and of all the tomorrows to come. He thought of his legs.

The next morning Megan awoke to the sound of music. She was alone; Ricardo had already gone. She groaned and buried her head in the pillow, wondering who had turned a radio on so early. Then it occurred to her that it was live music.

She looked at the bedside clock. It was six-thirty. What in the world? She sat up, swung her legs off the bed and reached for her robe just as Pilar knocked and ran into the room.

"It's mariachis, Mom," Pilar said excitedly. "You're being serenaded!" She grabbed Megan's arm. "Hurry up! They're right outside in your garden."

"But how did they...?" Megan pulled back the curtains and opened the French doors. The musician closest to her bowed from the waist, then turned to the other musicians and gave them a signal to stop.

"Buenos días," he said. Then he bowed again and said to the musicians, *"¡Ahora, sí!"*

They began to play "Strangers in the Night," and one of them, a handsome gray-haired man began to sing.

"I never heard that song before," Pilar whispered.

"It's an old song, sweetheart." Megan smiled. "It was popular when your dad and I first met."

It was the song Ricardo had serenaded her with the morning after their first date. A love song. And he had remembered.

Megan put her hand on Pilar's shoulder, and together they listened while the mariachis sang the old, but, oh, so sweetly remembered song of love.

In the *sorteo* he drew the sixth and last bull of the day, a *castaño,* a chestnut-colored animal, with a wide spread of horns.

"Let's hope he's as brave as he is strong," Juan Larrea said when the number was drawn. "He's *mucho toro,* Ricardo. You'll have to be careful of him."

They went back to the hotel so that he could rest. He had eaten only a light breakfast before the *sorteo,* and he wouldn't eat again until after the corrida. This was the way it was, one of the rules. A matador's stomach must be almost empty in case of immediate surgery.

At three he dressed in his suit of lights. It was a new one that he had only recently had made—silver and a shade of blue the same color as Megan's eyes and decorated with ornate braid and silver trim.

The *taleguilla,* the breeches, were skintight so there would be no fold or drape of material that a horn could catch on. With it he wore the white ruffled bull-fighter's shirt, a narrow red tie and a red sash, a tight-fitting vest, a *chaquetilla*, a jacket, and the black heelless slippers.

When he was ready, his father pinned the *coleta*, the matador's braid of hair, to the back of his head. Then he embraced him and said, *"Suerte, Ricardo."*

At three-thirty one of his helpers brought the car around. He left the hotel, followed by shouts of "Good luck, Matador" from fans gathered in the lobby and on the street, and was driven to the Plaza Mexico, the largest bullring in the world. He said goodbye to his father and to Juan Larrea there and went to the passageway below the ring where he would wait with the other matadors who would fight today.

Arturo Cruz and Enrique Alcazar smoked. Vicente Cano had a whispered consultation with his manager. Curro Mejias fussed with his *capote de paseo,* the ornately embroidered cape that all of the matadors wore draped over their left shoulders. Ricardo smoothed his own *capote* with the richly embroidered image of *La Guadalupana*. Felipe Guzman looked straight ahead and spoke to no one.

The music of the *paso doble* began. Cruz and Alcazar put out their cigarettes. Curro Mejias bowed his head and made the sign of the cross.

The *alguacil,* dressed in black velvet and wearing a plumed hat, rode into the ring to just below the president of the bullfight's box and doffed his hat. The president nodded, and a helper in the *callejon,* the passageway between the fence and the seating area, handed the *aguacil* the symbolic key to give to the *torilero,* the man who would open the gate from which the bulls would come.

The *alguacil* returned to the waiting matadors, and the glittering parade began. First came the matadors, followed by the banderilleros, the mounted picadors and the *monosabios,* who would help with the horses.

They stepped out into the sun and crossed the plaza, their backs straight, their faces serious. After they saluted the authority of the bullfight, they went to the place behind the *barrera* where they would stand.

Ricardo looked up to where Megan and Pilar were sitting with Isabel and Fernando. She and Pilar and Isabel held the carnations they would throw down to him if he made a tour of the ring. He took his *capote de paseo* and held it up so that Fernando could drape it over the front of their seats. Megan smiled down at him. Pilar called out, "Hi, Dad," and the people sitting near her laughed.

"She's your daughter?" Curro Mejias asked.

"Yes."

"She's beautiful."

Ricardo nodded. "Yes, she is."

The *monosabios* smoothed the sand.

A trumpet sounded.

Mejias, who would be first today, fixed his eyes upon the *toril,* the gate of fear from which the bull would come.

The gate swung open with a thud. And the bull, excited, wild, raging at having been penned up, surged like a thunderbolt into the ring.

The crowd cheered.

Mejias stepped out. *"¡Aha!"* he cried, and the bull raced toward him.

He did well. His cape lances were good. When it came time for the banderillas, he didn't do them; his helpers did. He did as well as he could with the red serge cloth, but his bull was difficult. When it came time to kill, Mejias missed his mark and it took four sword thrusts before the bull fell. By that time the crowd was booing. And Arturo Cruz, who stood watching next to Ricardo, looked up at them and muttered, "*¡Cabrones!* Can't they see he's doing his best?"

Vicente Cano fought next and received an ear. So did Arturo Cruz. Then came Enrique Alcazara, who started out well, but when he tried a *molinete,* a horn caught him. He was tossed and the calf of his leg ripped open. While his helpers called the bull away he limped to the side. A bandage was quickly wrapped around his wounded leg, but he had been hurt. He killed quickly, and when he left the ring to a smattering of applause, there was blood running down into his shoe.

Then it was Guzman's turn. Before the *toril* could open he ran out into the ring. Twelve feet from the gate he stopped, knelt and waited for the gate to open.

The bull exploded into the ring, stopped for only an instant, then, head down, bolted straight for Guzman. The matador held his ground, and at the last moment he swung the cape in a perfect *cambio afarolado.* Then another and another.

The crowd roared to its feet. "*¡Bravo!*" they shouted. "*¡Bravo!*"

Beside Ricardo, Vicente Cano muttered, "Son of a bitch."

Guzman was flashy and he was good. He was very good. His veronicas were flawless, his *delantal* perfect. But when it came time for the pic, he signaled for a longer pic than was necessary, weakening his animal so that it would be more obedient when he began to work with the muleta.

He did his own banderillas, the first pair good, the second pair misplaced. When it came time for the dedication, he dedicated the bull to the crowd.

His faena started off well, but because of the pic his bull lacked endurance. And though Guzman tried a variety of passes, none of them quite came off, and twice the animal went to its knees.

When it was time to kill, he did well and was awarded an ear.

Now it was Ricardo's turn. He looked toward the gate. It opened, and his animal, twelve hundred pounds of infuriated muscle, raced into the ring.

Ricardo didn't step out immediately. Instead he waited, watching as his helpers tested his animal's movements with their capes. And when he was satisfied, he stepped out into the ring.

He thought of nothing now except the bull, he and this magnificent animal, alone in this giant arena.

He called out to it, *"¡Toro! ¡Aha, Toro!"* and it came, horns flashing in the sun, straight for his body. He didn't move except for that small flicker of the cape when it reached him, and it passed so close that he could smell animal sweat and urine.

He passed the bull again and again. He didn't move his feet, but stood as though rooted to the ground, drawing the bull closer and still closer to his body.

And when he finished his series with a media-veronica, he turned his back on the animal and signaled for the picadors.

He allowed only two soft pics instead of the usual three. This was a wonderful animal; he wouldn't ruin it as Guzman had ruined his.

"Brilliant!" his father said when he went back to stand behind the *barrera*. "I've never seen you do better."

The crowd began to whistle, an indication that they wanted Ricardo to do his own banderillas.

"Let the banderilleros do it," Juan Larrea said. "Save yourself for the faena."

"No." Ricardo motioned for one of his men to give him the first pair of sticks. "Today I must do everything."

"But your legs—"

Ricardo rested his hand on Larrea's shoulder. "Don't worry, my friend. My legs will be all right."

He would make them be all right. He would will them to be strong.

"You did as I asked?" he questioned Larrea.

"*Sí, Matador.* But are you sure?"

"I am sure."

He stepped back into the ring. His helpers had placed the bull well back into the center of the ring. He and the bull regarded each other. "*¡Aha!*" Ricardo shouted, and began his zigzag run toward the animal, close, closer, now up, plant the sticks, and pivot away from the horns. In time. Just in time.

They were perfect, and so were the next two pair.

He went back to the *barrera* and rinsed his mouth with water. Then he took his *montera,* the small black hat he and the other matadors had worn when they entered the ring, and after he asked permission to complete the third part of the fight, he went to stand below the row of seats where Megan and Pilar were seated.

They stood together, holding each other's hand.

"I dedicate this bull to the two of you," he said. "My wife and my daughter, with all the love that is in my heart." And, turning his back, he tossed his *montera* up to them.

Megan caught it and clutched it to her breast as he stepped back into the ring to begin this final portion of the corrida.

He called the bull to him and began a series of stunningly beautiful passes. The people around Megan cried out, *"¡Bravo! ¡Mucho!"* And when Megan looked at them, she saw the excitement on their faces, their passion for this art of bullfighting, and knew when she looked back at the ring that she was seeing the perfect performance by the perfect matador.

For the first time she understood Ricardo's love of what he did. She saw his beauty and his grace, his artistry and his skill. His art.

He completed a series of passes, and when he turned his back on the bull, he looked up to that section of the arena where the band was and motioned to them.

They began to play, and suddenly the crowd was on its feet, screaming, "No! No! Don't do this! No!"

"What is it?" Megan turned to Fernando. "What's happening?"

"You knew nothing of this?"

"Of what? I don't understand."

"They're playing 'Las Golondrinas,' the song of farewell."

"Of farewell?"

"It means Ricardo is leaving the ring." Isabel began to cry. "It's his farewell, Megan. This is the last time he'll fight."

Megan looked down into the ring. Ricardo's face was expressionless. He didn't look at her.

She didn't know she was weeping until Pilar said, "Don't cry, Mom. Please don't cry."

She felt such a mixture of emotions. She was glad, oh, so glad this would be the last fight, but mixed with her happiness was sorrow for what he was giving up. She knew his pain, she felt his pain, and yes, at last she understood what all of this meant to him.

The red cape flared against the sun as Ricardo drew the bull closer and yet closer. He was grace and elegance of motion, the supreme matador, a man who had dared everything, a man brave enough to stop when he knew it was time.

The crowd grew silent, and all that was heard in the giant arena was the soft cry of *"¡Aha, Toro! ¡Aha!"* And the sad sweet strains of the song of farewell:

Where wilt thou go, my agile little swallow?
Thy wings wilt tire if long thy flight should be.
If wind and storm should bring thee pain and anguish,
If seeking shelter, none be found for thee.

I leave the land that is to me beloved,
That gave me birth, for some bleak distant shore.
A poor lone wand'rer 'mid sharp pain and anguish,
I leave my home, and can return no more.
And can return no more.

This was the last time, the last bull. The best bull of his career, following where he led, brave and true, courageous to the end.

His legs quivered with strain.

It had to end, yet he didn't want it to end.

He looked up at the crowd. He heard them call, "*¡Toro, Toro, Toro!*" He saw the white handker-chiefs and knew they wanted him to save this bull. He made one more pass, then another and another. Then he stepped back and nodded, acceding to the wishes of the crowd.

When he went to the *barrera,* his father, his face distorted with anger and disbelief, demanded, "Why? Why are you doing this?"

"Because it's time," Ricardo said. "Will you cut the *coleta?*"

"I don't want to." Franco hesitated. "But if it's what you want..."

"It's what I want."

Father and son stepped out from behind the fence. The crowd rose to its feet and watched while Franco clipped the small black pigtail from the back of Ri-cardo's head.

When it was done, they gave him the trophy, the prized Estoque de Oro.

Juan Larrea and the men of Ricardo's cuadrilla came to stand beside him. Their faces, all except for Larrea, who had known this was what Ricardo had planned, were stunned. Together they began to make the circle of the ring.

The crowd threw roses and carnations. They threw wineskins, and when Ricardo stopped and held one up to drink from, they roared their approval.

At last he reached the place where Megan and Pilar waited. He looked up and saw that Megan was weep-ing and that her face, though tear-stained, was filled with love. Then she and Pilar and Isabel threw their red carnations down to him, and he gathered them up in his arms.

He went into the center of the ring for that one last, final bow. Still holding the flowers, he crossed his arms over his chest in a gesture that said, "I love you. I love you all." As he turned, encompassing all of them, he sought out one face in the crowd. And when he found it, he knew that what he was doing was right, for her and for him: "If wind and storm should bring thee pain and anguish, If seeking shelter, none be found for thee..."

It is over, Ricardo thought, but it will be all right. For I have found my shelter. I have found my love.

* * * * *

SILHOUETTE·INTIMATE·MOMENTS

COMING NEXT MONTH

#433 UNFINISHED BUSINESS—Nora Roberts

When sexy, successful Vanessa Sexton returned to her hometown for some rest and relaxation, she didn't expect to run into Dr. Brady Tucker—the only man she'd ever loved. He had broken her heart years ago—how could she ever let him back into her life now?

#434 WAKE TO DARKNESS—Blythe Stephens

Curtis Macklin's investigation of a shot in the night offered him an opportunity he couldn't pass up—the elegant Yvonne Worthington. Certain she would lead him to his fiancée's murderer, he came to her rescue. But vulnerable Yvonne had lost her memory, and suddenly Curtis's priorities changed. He had to keep her safe from the bad guys...and himself.

#435 TRUE TO THE FIRE—Suzanne Carey

Revolutionary leader Gabriel Sanchez could handle many things. Unfortunately, protecting Miranda Burton was not one of them. She could never fit into his dangerous world, so being true to his cause meant rejecting love as a luxury he couldn't afford—or could he?

#436 WITHOUT WARNING—Ann Williams

Michael Baldwin—alive? Blair Mallory couldn't believe her childhood sweetheart had survived the boating accident ten years ago. Now Michael was back and wanted to avenge his father's death. But this Michael wasn't the same man Blair once knew—this dangerous stranger was tough and mean and oh, so sexy. This man, without warning, could steal her heart once again....

AVAILABLE THIS MONTH:

#429 NOW YOU SEE HIM...
Ann Stuart

#430 DEFYING GRAVITY
Rachel Lee

#431 L.A. MIDNIGHT
Rebecca Daniels

#432 THE MATADOR
Barbara Faith

NORA ROBERTS

Love has a language all its own, and for centuries, flowers have symbolized love's finest expression. Discover the language of flowers—and love—in this romantic collection of 48 favorite books by bestselling author Nora Roberts.

Two titles are available each month at your favorite retail outlet.

In May, look for:

Night Moves, **Volume #7**
Dance of Dreams, **Volume #8**

In June, look for:

Opposites Attract, **Volume #9**
Island of Flowers, **Volume #10**

Collect all 48 titles
and become fluent in

THE LANGUAGE of LOVE

 Silhouette ®

"GET AWAY FROM IT ALL" SWEEPSTAKES

HERE'S HOW THE SWEEPSTAKES WORKS

NO PURCHASE NECESSARY

o enter each drawing, complete the appropriate Official Entry Form or a 3" by
" index card by hand-printing your name, address and phone number and
e trip destination that the entry is being submitted for (i.e., Caneel Bay,
anyon Ranch or London and the English Countryside) and mailing it to: Get
way From It All Sweepstakes, P.O. Box 1397, Buffalo, New York 14269-1397.

o responsibility is assumed for lost, late or misdirected mail. Entries must be
ent separately with first class postage affixed, and be received by: 4/15/92
r the Caneel Bay Vacation Drawing, 5/15/92 for the Canyon Ranch Vacation
rawing and 6/15/92 for the London and the English Countryside Vacation
rawing. Sweepstakes is open to residents of the U.S. (except Puerto Rico)
nd Canada, 21 years of age or older as of 5/31/92.

r complete rules send a self-addressed, stamped (WA residents need not
fix return postage) envelope to: Get Away From It All Sweepstakes, P.O. Box
892, Blair, NE 68009.

1992 HARLEQUIN ENTERPRISES LTD.   SWP-RLS

"GET AWAY FROM IT ALL" SWEEPSTAKES

HERE'S HOW THE SWEEPSTAKES WORKS

NO PURCHASE NECESSARY

 enter each drawing, complete the appropriate Official Entry Form or a 3" by
 index card by hand-printing your name, address and phone number and
e trip destination that the entry is being submitted for (i.e., Caneel Bay,
anyon Ranch or London and the English Countryside) and mailing it to: Get
way From It All Sweepstakes, P.O. Box 1397, Buffalo, New York 14269-1397.

 responsibility is assumed for lost, late or misdirected mail. Entries must be
nt separately with first class postage affixed, and be received by: 4/15/92
r the Caneel Bay Vacation Drawing, 5/15/92 for the Canyon Ranch Vacation
awing and 6/15/92 for the London and the English Countryside Vacation
awing. Sweepstakes is open to residents of the U.S. (except Puerto Rico)
d Canada, 21 years of age or older as of 5/31/92.

r complete rules send a self-addressed, stamped (WA residents need not
fix return postage) envelope to: Get Away From It All Sweepstakes, P.O. Box
92, Blair, NE 68009.

1992 HARLEQUIN ENTERPRISES LTD.   SWP-RLS

"GET AWAY FROM IT ALL"

Brand-new Subscribers-Only Sweepstakes

OFFICIAL ENTRY FORM

This entry must be received by: May 15, 1992
This month's winner will be notified by: May 31, 1992
Trip must be taken between: June 30, 1992—June 30, 1993

YES, I want to win the Canyon Ranch vacation for two. I understand the prize includes round-trip airfare and the two additional prizes revealed in the BONUS PRIZES insert.

Name _____

Address _____

City _____

State/Prov._____ Zip/Postal Code_____

Daytime phone number _____
(Area Code)

Return entries with invoice in envelope provided. Each book in this shipment has two entry coupons — and the more coupons you enter, the better your chances of winning!
© 1992 HARLEQUIN ENTERPRISES LTD.   2M-CPN